D1559343

The Case of the Constant Caller

FATHER DOWLING MYSTERIES
by Ralph McInerny

Her Death of Cold
The Seventh Station
Bishop as Pawn
Lying Three
Second Vespers
Thicker Than Water
A Loss of Patients
The Grass Widow
Getting A Way With Murder
Rest in Pieces
The Basket Case
Abracadaver
Four on the Floor
Judas Priest
Desert Sinner
Seed of Doubt
A Cardinal Offense

The Case of the Constant Caller

A FATHER DOWLING MYSTERY
FOR YOUNG ADULTS

Ralph McInerny

St. Martin's Press
New York

For Terrill

ISBN 0-312-13037-6

First Edition: June 1995

10 9 8 7 6 5 4 3 2 1

1

Janet took the summer job because she had no choice. How was she supposed to know that then she'd meet Gerry Krause?

What had once been St. Hilary's school was now a center where the older parishioners could spend their day, visiting with one another, playing cards or shuffleboard, or taking part in one of the activities planned by Edna Hospers. Janet Hospers's job was to help her mother run programs for the old folks.

"Doing what?" her friend Beth had asked, wrinkling her nose. Beth still hadn't found a job, but she acted as if she'd rather have none at all than do what Janet was doing.

"Just helping out. You know."

"But I don't know. You'll be working for your mother?"

That seemed to make it less than a real job. Working with old people and working for her mother—there were two strikes against the job. That was before she started, so she hadn't yet met Gerry Krause, but even if she had she wouldn't have mentioned him to Beth. With boys you never knew, but she knew enough not to assume that the ones you like like you. It was her second day when Father Dowling called out to her as she was playing shuffleboard with old Mr. Walsh. The boy with Father Dowling was a head taller than the priest. He looked about as embarrassed as she did as they came across the schoolyard toward her.

"You wanna get in the game, Father?" Mr. Walsh asked.

"This is Gerry Krause, Janet. Would you show him around?" And Father Dowling took her shuffleboard cue and joined Mr. Walsh.

Janet surprised herself by the way she explained to Gerry how the school was used now. In the auditorium, her mother was herding together those who were going on the excursion to the museum. No point in bothering her now. The lower corridor of the school was still lined with the class photographs from past years, the latest one fifteen years old.

"Where do you go to school?" she asked when they stopped to get Cokes from a machine.

"De la Salle."

She looked at him. "Where's that?"

"Minneapolis."

"What are you doing in Fox River?"

"Visiting my uncle."

"Father Dowling?"

He laughed. Janet felt small beside him. He was over six feet tall, his hair was in a crew cut, and his eyes crinkled nicely when he smiled. He was the kind of boy she admired from a distance at school, despairing of ever catching their eye. But Gerry seemed just another boy—tall, very good-looking, a little awkward, as if he felt ill at ease with her. Not that he wasn't interested in being shown around. It was almost embarrassing the way he took it all in.

"How long will be you be visiting?"

"That depends."

"On what?"

His face clouded. "On my parents."

Of course she didn't press him on it, but it made her feel closer to him. Not that she would ever tell him about her dad.

"The reason I'm here, at St. Hilary's, my uncle said Father Dowling might have some things for me to do around here."

"Around the school!"

"I don't think so. He said yardwork, mainly."

A man named Fisk mowed and trimmed, when he was sober. He was one of the pastor's protégés. Janet had heard all about him from her mother. Fisk sometimes just disappeared, and if the grass got cut at all then it was not by Fisk. But Father Dowling never took the opportunity to get rid of him.

"He can't bear to fire anyone."

Mrs. Murkin, the housekeeper, had done her best to convince Father Dowling to get rid of Fisk. The solution seemed to be to hire Gerry and keep on Fisk as well.

"Mrs. Murkin says she doubts we'll ever see him again," Gerry told her.

"What does Father Dowling say?"

"Not to listen to Mrs. Murkin."

Throughout that first afternoon, Janet kept thinking of how she'd tell Beth about the boy who would also be working at St. Hilary's. Or maybe she wouldn't make an announcement, as if it were a big deal. She'd just let mention of him slip out sometime and enjoy Beth's reaction.

"Oh, haven't I mentioned him? He's nice."

But most of the time she was absorbed in taking Gerry around the school. When they came outside again, he asked how long she'd worked there.

"I'm new this summer," she said. What would he have thought if she told him this was her second day?

Mr. Walsh scowled as Father Dowling blasted his marker off a numbered square. "I thought you said you never played before!" Mr. Walsh whined.

"You asked me if I was any good, not whether I had played before."

"You said you were an amateur."

"Lucky," the priest said, handing the stick to Janet.

"Who was that?" her mother asked when they were on their way home.

"He's going to help out with the yardwork."

"He is? What about Fisk?"

"I don't know."

"I didn't know Father Dowling was looking for anyone."

"Things just turned out that way. He's here on a visit."

"Where is he from?"

"Minneapolis."

Her mother's surprised eyes were briefly on Janet. "Is he visiting Father Dowling?"

Janet laughed. "That's what I thought. No, he's staying with his uncle. Apparently his parents are having some kind of trouble."

"He told you that?"

"Yes."

Her mother looked as if she had given up trying to understand the young. Didn't they keep anything secret?

"What is his name?"

"Gerry. Gerry Krause. His uncle is Captain Keegan."

"Keegan!"

It took a minute for Janet to understand her mother's reaction. Captain Keegan was the man who'd arrested her father.

* * *

As the eldest, Janet remembered her father better than her two brothers did, but none of her memories of him suggested a man who had done the things that had put him in prison for the rest of his life. That didn't mean the rest of his life, of course—her mother always added that whenever she spoke of it, which wasn't often. A visitor might have thought her father was in the army, or he was an astronaut off on a long voyage. Her father would be an old man when he was released.

"And she's waiting for him?" Beth asked.

"Of course."

"I wouldn't. Would you? I mean, after all, it's his fault he's there—isn't it?—so he more or less deserted your mother and you kids."

"What do you suggest?"

Luckily, Beth caught the tone of her voice and dropped it. Their friendship had survived lots of things, but this time Beth had come closest to saying something unforgivable. Not that Janet hadn't thought of it herself. Her parents were separated indefinitely, so why not make it formal? Catholics can't get a divorce—or at least they don't think divorce really ends the marriage—but there are annulments. Mrs. Murkin had made the mistake of bringing up that topic with her mother, so Janet knew what the reaction was. What kept her mother loyal to her absent, imprisoned father? For Janet, that was one of the great mysteries of life.

"I love him," her mother said, repeating what she had said to Mrs. Murkin. To Janet she added, "He's your father and my husband, and nothing can change that. Nothing will. I married him for better or worse."

And got the worse? It sure looked that way. Her father was a voice on the audiotapes he sent home when her mother went to visit. His main concern seemed to be that they should know about his parents, who had died when he was young but who had been the best people in the world and they were never to think otherwise. And he wanted them to know where the Hospers had come from. He had lots of time to look into his family tree, and that was what he was doing. He did not want any of the kids to visit him and see him as a prisoner. It made Janet all the more determined that she would one day go to Joliet, with or without her mother, and visit with her father and prove to him that she loved him.

"What kind of trouble are his parents having?" her mother asked.

"He didn't say."

2

Whenever his parents fought, Gerry would get on his bike and just ride, and if things weren't over when he got home he would stay outside, chipping balls with a wedge, pretending he was a million miles away. It was bad, but he had never imagined they would actually ever declare a truce and say the war was over. His mother cried and his father asked to meet him and they went to a McDonald's where they sat at a plastic table and his father tried to explain to him why he was leaving his mother and Gerry and Maureen.

"These things happen, Gerry."

A kid was mopping the floor, and the place was only half full in the middle of the afternoon. Gerry hadn't been hungry, but he ate with concentration so he wouldn't have to look at his father.

"Some day you'll understand. Of course, you can't now, anymore than I could have when I was your age."

His father looked away, his eyes damp, but he was feeling sorry for himself. It was tough telling your own son you were leaving his mother for another woman.

Gerry suddenly felt older than his father. He couldn't imagine either of his grandfathers doing what his dad was doing. What would Uncle Phil Keegan say when he heard what was going on? At the time, Gerry still hoped that this was just a temporary thing, something that could be fixed, maybe by his father having a good talk with Uncle Phil. He didn't believe that anymore, but when his mother arranged to spend a month with her parents, taking Maureen along, Gerry had asked if he could visit Uncle Phil. It had seemed a mistake until he got the job at St. Hilary's.

If his uncle had suggested he work for a priest before Gerry met Father Dowling he would have turned it down flat. But the three of them went to a Cubs game and afterward went back to the rectory and watched the White Sox on television while Mrs. Murkin kept bringing him things to eat.

"I'd bring you a gas mask but you couldn't wear it and eat at the same time."

Mrs. Murkin made a big thing of the pastor's pipe and Captain Keegan's cigar.

"Close the door, Marie," the pastor said.

"You afraid some smoke will get out?"

"It's what gets in."

Captain Keegan laughed, Mrs. Murkin shut the door noisily, and Gerry felt right at home, one of the guys. Why wasn't his father more like Uncle Phil?

"So what am I going to do with Gerry, Roger?" his uncle asked Father Dowling. "He's not old enough to put on the force."

"And there's the intelligence test."

"Oh, he's dumb enough." Uncle Phil punched Gerry on the arm.

"He can work here."

"With the old folks in the school?"

"Maybe helping Fisk."

"Fisk!"

"Fisk is a jack of all trades, Gerry. He could use help with the lawns and hedges and the like. There's a tractor mower, but he's afraid to use it."

It had been arranged that easily. For minimum wage Gerry would see that the lawns were mowed and the hedges kept trimmed and the grounds well watered. And he could have Wednesday afternoons as well as the weekends off.

"I wouldn't mind the job myself," Uncle Phil said.

"Fisk wouldn't have you."

"Fisk!"

Fisk dressed like a kid—in jeans, T-shirt, and sweatband—but his hair was going gray, his skin was leathery, and there were tattoos on his upper arms. He just nodded when Father Dowling introduced Gerry, then took him off to the maintenance shed and showed him the tractor mower.

"Ever use one of those?"

Gerry walked around the machine. It hardly looked used. "I can handle it."

"It was his idea. To make things easier." Fisk's tone was sarcastic. "The first time I tried it I ran into a tree. The second time I cut a path through a flowerbed. The damned thing's a menace."

Gerry was beginning to understand why Father Dowling had hired him.

"Let me give it a try."

"I'll be over in the school."

Fisk left the maintenance shed and hurried toward the school as if he were washing his hands of the whole thing. Gerry found the book on the tractor and paged through it before starting the motor. He backed the tractor out of the shed and onto the lawn, where he lowered the blade, put it in gear, and started mowing. He went back and forth on the lawn, and soon Fisk appeared and stood in the shade by the school, watching. He had his thumbs hooked in his pockets, and he surveyed the scene as if his personal orders were being executed. When he waved him over, Gerry put the tractor in neutral and went to Fisk.

"You think it's safe leaving it on like that?"

"It's not going anywhere."

"Okay. That's your job, kid. But let me give you some advice. Take it easy. Nothing around here has to be done in a hurry, understand? Say you mow that lawn once a week. You don't want to get it all done in a day."

The parish plant covered three acres, but the church and parish house and school accounted for much of that, to say nothing of the parking lot. Still there were three distinct areas of lawn: in front of the school, around the parish house, and on the far side of the church. Hoses and sprinklers had to be taken from one lawn to another. The hedges and flowerbeds were less demanding. Within a few hours Gerry could see how his week would go.

Father Dowling said Mass at noon and asked Gerry to have lunch with him afterward.

"Couldn't Fisk come?" the priest asked, winking. He got the reaction from the housekeeper that he wanted.

It was a great lunch, during which the pastor told Gerry what a wonderful uncle he had.

"We've become close friends. Since your aunt died we spend a lot of time together. Did he ever tell you he wanted to be a priest when he was young?"

"It's a good thing he didn't," Mrs. Murkin said. She came and went but obviously considered herself part of the conversation.

"Mrs. Murkin likes eligible widowers."

The kitchen door slammed behind the housekeeper.

Afterward Father Dowling took Gerry to the school and introduced him to Janet Hospers.

"Not bad," Fisk said when Gerry left her, after getting a tour of the school.

"Father Dowling said you would show me around your domain."

"Domain!" He scowled, but Gerry thought Fisk liked the suggestion that he was in command. "I knew her father."

"Janet's?"

"Yeah."

"What happened to him? Is he dead?"

"Oh no, nothing so bad as that."

Gerry wondered if he and Janet had that in common: a father who had tired of his family and left.

3

Mrs. Murkin had been housekeeper at St. Hilary's parish in Fox River, Illinois, long before Roger Dowling had been appointed pastor. With such seniority, it was understandable that she sometimes felt that she was in charge. Father Dowling was a terrible tease, but she had grown used to him. To anyone but him she would admit that he was the best pastor the parish had ever had. When Captain Keegan became such a crony of the pastor, she was not sure she approved. The two liked nothing better than to hole up in the pastor's study and watch a game on television, filling the room with smoke. But Phil Keegan spoke freely of what was going on in the detective division of the Fox River police, and Marie soon found that compensation enough for the mess the two made. She considered it part of her duties to listen in. That is how she heard of the release of Patrick Crowe.

"It's the plea bargaining, Roger. They could have nailed him with first-degree murder, but he pled guilty to second and now he's free as a bird."

"On parole."

Phil Keegan shrugged this away as an inconvenience.

"You were the arresting officer, weren't you, Phil?"

"And chief witness. It was the prosecutor who made the deal."

"Who does a man like that resent most, the officer who arrests him or the prosecutor?"

Keegan looked at the priest. "Did Cy Horvath tell you about Crowe?"

"Tell me what?"

Marie sat down to listen to the story. Crowe had been involved in sophisticated theft, robbing local electronic warehouses of computer parts, which he then sold in the Third World at enormous profits. In seeking a pattern for the thefts, Keegan had looked for someone connected with the apparently random break-ins. Crowe was a salesman for a company that manufactured relatively simple components, but his calls gave him access to the information required to make possible the break-ins. When the police were closing in on Crowe and he must have known the end was near, a man with a record as a burglar was found dead. Establishing that the dead man was Crowe's accomplice linked him to the murder, but in the end Crowe pled guilty to manslaughter and went off to a long prison sentence, but with the possibility of parole. Before he left he taunted Horvath to give a message to Keegan: "Next time it won't be manslaughter." The threat, while veiled, was clear. And now Crowe had been released from prison.

It gave Marie Murkin the shivers, and that night, when she climbed the back stairs to her quarters over the kitchen, she made certain the windows were locked and the blinds pulled before she settled down to read a while before turning off the light. How a person living in a parish house could feel insecure was difficult to say, but what Phil Keegan had said about Crowe seemed to touch St. Hilary's too. After all, Edna

Hospers's husband was in prison because of the efforts of Phil Keegan. And Father Dowling had insisted on hiring that ne'er-do-well Willy Fisk, whom anyone could tell had not put in an honest day's work in his life. Priests and ministers were soft touches for vagrants and the shiftless—Marie knew all about that—but it was one thing to give a man a meal and a few dollars and send him on his way and another to let him set himself up in the basement of the school and call himself the maintenance man. And now Father Dowling had hired Phil Keegan's nephew to do Fisk's work for him. Honestly. Marie hadn't read a word before she turned off the light, but she lay sleepless for half an hour, thinking of the odd assortment of people Father Dowling had surrounded himself with.

Edna Hospers was worth her weight in gold. Marie had said it before and she meant it. Edna's independence was a little hard to bear—the suggestion that she and Marie Murkin were equals before the pastor, if indeed Edna were not in a superior position! The former school turned into a parish center drew dozens of older parishioners every day, and under Edna's direction it had flourished, no doubt about that. She was always adding new things for her charges to do: taking them on excursions in the minibus, arranging evenings of entertainment, and—an inspiration—arranging a program put on by the old people themselves that had been a great hit. Marie smiled indulgently in the dark at the thought. It seldom occurred to her that she herself was as old as half of those who came to the center. Maybe it would never have occurred to her if Tim Walsh hadn't broadcast to the world that they had been in school together.

"She was only a class or two ahead of me," he had brayed.

She shook the memory away and thought of Janet. Edna's daughter. What a lovely girl. She had the maturity of a girl with two younger brothers. Who would even suspect she was the daughter of a man who . . .

The thought trailed away as the image of Gerry and Janet talking together formed in Marie's mind. Would the boy be interested in Janet if he knew? Working together every day, Marie was certain that the two were destined to be more than acquaintances, and she dreaded it. Or were they perhaps destined not to become friendly because of Janet's father? It seemed clear to Marie that Janet faced a dilemma. Whether or not she told Gerry of her father, she ran the risk of turning him away. Immediately, if she told him; later and more painfully, if he found out from someone else.

Marie was able to fall asleep only when she resolved to put the matter to Father Dowling in the morning.

4

Gerry was mowing on the far side of the church when the car pulled up to the curb and a man got out and made it clear he wanted to talk. Even in neutral, the tractor made an awful racket, so Gerry turned the key.

"Thanks, kid, I appreciate it. This St. Hilary's parish?"

"That's right. If you want to see Father Dowling . . ."

"Whoa," the man said, holding up a hand. "I wanna see a priest, I got my own." He grinned as if he had told a joke. "You work for the parish, right?"

"Yes."

"Know a man named Fisk?"

The man reminded Gerry of Fisk, even though the stranger was dressed in a suit and wore a straw hat. There was a cigarette in the corner of his mouth, and he looked as if he belonged on a grade-school playground, despite the fact that, like Fisk, he was middle-aged.

"He's over in the school."

"The school?"

"That's where he lives."

"He lives there?"

"He has an apartment in the basement. Look, I'll go get him."

"No, no. Wait. Fact is, I don't have time right now. I just wanted to know if he worked here."

"I can tell him you were asking for him."

The man's eyes narrowed, and he shook his head. "Naw. I'd rather surprise him. Here." He pulled some money from his pocket and peeled off a dollar bill, hesitated, then peeled off another and handed them to Gerry.

"I can't take that."

"Something wrong with my money?"

"I haven't done anything to earn it."

"Weren't you going to help me surprise my old friend?" The man pushed the money into Gerry's shirt pocket. "What's your name, kid?"

"Gerry Krause."

"How'd you get the job?"

"My uncle Captain Keegan knows Father Dowling. . . ."

The man stepped back as if Gerry had struck him. The squint-eyed wise-guy look was gone, and his mouth had dropped open.

"Keegan?"

"That's right."

"No kidding? I once knew a man named Keegan."

He had regained his jaunty air as he slipped behind the wheel of the car. He looked up at Gerry. "Remember, don't tell Fisk."

Gerry said nothing, and in a moment the car pulled away and took off up the street with squealing tires. He even drove like a kid.

Riding a tractor mower gives you lots of time to think, and for the next hour Gerry thought about the man in the car and his strange question about Fisk and his stranger reaction when he heard the name Keegan. Gerry had an idea that it was his uncle that the man had once known. Before he'd finished mowing he decided that he ought to tell Fisk about the man.

Fisk took his time opening the door of his room, then stood gripping the frame, eyes bloodshot, face unshaven, staring out at Gerry. But he woke up when Gerry told him about the man in the car.

"What'd he look like?"

Gerry described the suit and the straw hat better than he could the man's expression. He decided not to say that the man had reminded him of Fisk.

"Come on in while I put on coffee."

Fisk put his head out the door and looked up and down the hall before closing the door and locking it. His place smelled of alcohol and was a mess besides. In the kitchenette, he ran water into a coffeepot and picked up a beer can and drank from it. Once he got the coffee on, he sat Gerry down and wanted to hear everything he could remember about the man who had questioned him. What kind of car was he driving? Did he notice the license plates? Was there anyone else in the car? Gerry surprised himself by how much he remembered. The car was an Olds, it had Illinois plates, there had been no one else in the car—no one visible, at any rate.

"His shoes were real flashy. Brown and white, with holes in them."

"Holes?"

"Little holes punched in the leather."

"You mean perforated?"

"Okay, perforated. He rocked from side to side when he talked, and looked kind of bowlegged."

Fisk stared at him. "Who trained you, your uncle?"

"Trained me?"

"It's unnatural to notice so much. You sure you're not making it up?"

"Why would I make it up?"

"I don't know. Do you always remember everything you see, or was it just this guy?"

Even as he said this, it was clear Fisk did not want to think that his visitor had made such an indelible impression on Gerry.

"Do you know who he was?" Gerry asked.

Fisk's eyes narrowed, as his visitor's had. "Naw. It could be anyone."

"You'd better be careful."

"What do you mean?"

"He said he wanted to surprise you. He looked like a practical joker to me."

Fisk slumped into a chair, holding a mug of coffee in both hands. He seemed to have aged right before Gerry's eyes. "Who is he, Willy?"

Fisk's eyes lifted, then moved away. "One of my old classmates."

"From high school?" It seemed unlikely that Fisk had gone beyond high school, if he had gotten that far.

Fisk emitted a little barking laugh. "We were classmates at Joliet."

A college? Gerry wouldn't have believed it.

"Look," Fisk said, getting to his feet. "If you see him around again, let me know right away, okay?"

There was a tap on the door, and Fisk spun toward it. After a moment of silence, he said, "See who that is, will you, Gerry?"

When Gerry opened the door, old Mr. Walsh was standing there wearing a devilish expression, but when he saw Gerry it faded away.

"Willy here?"

"That you, Tim?" Fisk had gotten out of sight behind Gerry but now came into view. "Come in, come in. I was just giving Gerry his marching orders. He'll be on his way. I suppose you've come for a cup of coffee?"

"That depends on what you put in it."

Gerry left, closing the door on the chuckling older men. Working at St. Hilary's made him realize how oddly young the old are.

5

"Has he asked you out?"

Janet looked at Beth. *"Out?* We see one another all day!"

"How romantic."

"Have you found a job yet?" Janet asked. The best defense is a good offense, as Gerry had said when they were talking about Mrs. Murkin.

The room Gerry lived in was on the pastor's side of the house. Long before, when the parish had flourished, it had been the room of an assistant pastor. To hear Gerry tell it, Mrs. Murkin was as nosy as Beth.

"What's she ask about?"

"Everything."

"But like what?"

The way he acted Janet was sure that Mrs. Murkin had been asking him about her and her family, and she felt a sudden chill. Would the housekeeper tell Gerry about her father? Her reaction to that possibility told her that she did not want him hearing it from anyone but her. So she told him, quickly, cleanly, completely.

"How long ago was that?"

"I was seven years old. Nine years ago."

"How often do you get to see him?"

She didn't want to tell him that she had never visited her

father during all these years. He said he couldn't bear to have his children see him in prison, and Janet had come to understand that. Her father's tragedy had brought them closer together: Janet, her brothers, her mother. They were the custodians of a terrible secret. They had moved into a new neighborhood, and not even Beth knew the whole truth about her father. Now Janet had told Gerry and she was glad she had. His reaction was just right, surprised but sympathetic too.

"Where is he?"

"Joliet."

Gerry's eyes grew large. "Is that a prison?"

"Yes."

He shook his head. "Was Willy Fisk there?"

Janet didn't know. When she asked her mother, there was a tense silence. "Why do you ask?"

"Someone said he was."

"Someone?"

"Gerry Krause."

"Does he know about your father too?"

"I told him."

"You did!"

"I didn't want him hearing it from someone else and thinking we were ashamed or something."

"Are you sure he didn't already know?"

"Of course he didn't know. That's why I told him. And then he said that Willy Fisk had been there."

"And where did he learn that?"

"I didn't ask."

"Probably from Captain Keegan."

It was the first time Janet was aware of her mother's feelings toward Gerry's uncle. Of course Captain Keegan must have been involved in the case. That her mother could have wished her father to go free no matter what he had done was perfectly understandable to Janet. She would have felt the same way. She felt now that if he could be released immediately to his family all would be well. Of course he had done terrible things, but perhaps many others who have done worse are walking the streets free. Why should it be thought necessary that a person should go on doing the wrong thing simply because of one mistake? Janet was certain that when her father was returned to them, he would be good in every way and the bitter past would be erased from his memory. In that happy future it would be possible to tell everyone what once had been but was not now.

Beth had asked about dating for a reason. Nick Stafford was working as a bagger at the supermarket, and Beth had been talking with him and one thing had led to another.

"He swims."

"Everybody swims."

Beth ignored this. "They have a cottage overlooking the Fox River, and they swim from their dock."

"Sounds like fun."

"That's what I said. I told him that if he had any sense of decency at all he would invite his friends over one of these hot summer nights."

"You didn't!"

"Yes, I did. Why not? He's our classmate, isn't he?"

He was also a cheerleader, class secretary, and very good-looking. But short. He was at least a head shorter than Beth.

"Well, congratulations."

"Oh, you're invited too, you and Gerry. I told Nick about you two and that you and I would make up a picnic."

"Beth, I am not going to ask Gerry out. We've just met, we work together, we're friends—that's all."

"It's a party, not a date-date. I'll ask him, if you won't."

"You will not."

"Will you?"

Even though she was mad at Beth for interfering, Janet thought what a nice excuse this was. It was only natural that, given the way they got along, she would dream of Gerry asking her out—to a movie, maybe to play tennis, something away from work. She felt at ease with him. The fact that they both had family troubles helped. That had made it possible for her to tell him of her father. All he'd said about his parents was that they had broken up, but the way he'd said it, the expression on his face, told her how much he had been hurt by it. The day after Beth's revelation about the swimming party at Nick Stafford's, Janet waited for the chance to bring it up.

In the morning, she drove the minibus to the mall to drop off three women who wanted to do some shopping. Driving the minibus to the mall or museum or wherever was a fun part of her job. As he often did, Mr. Walsh rode along, not going where the others were going but just for the ride.

"Most of my life I sat behind a desk, keeping accounts. I had a padded chair; I needed a cushion on that, and after a while nothing helped. I think if I had to stand for the rest of my life I could do it."

He stood in the aisle of the minibus, clutching a seatback in either hand, swaying with the movement of the vehicle. Janet just let him talk. Sooner or later an old person would tell you the story of their life. Mr. Walsh hadn't told her much, just that he had been an accountant.

"What company?"

"Oh, lots of them."

"Do you miss it?"

"Like a toothache."

"Have you lived in St. Hilary's all your life?"

"I don't live there now."

Of course, it wasn't necessary to be a parishioner to use the center, but someone like Mr. Walsh was rare.

"How did you hear about it?"

"Word gets around."

At the mall, she let off her passengers, a trio of excited nervous grannies ready for a few hours of shopping with little prospect that they would buy anything. Janet supposed it brought back better days.

"I'll be right here at quarter of twelve, okay?"

"When did she say?"

"Twelve."

"A quarter of twelve," Janet shouted, leaning toward the open door. "Fifteen minutes before noon. Eleven-forty-five."

They nodded and moved away, still huddled together, looking brightly around them. Janet felt almost guilty leaving them on their own.

"Nonsense," Father Dowling said when she told him of it on her return to St. Hilary's. "You'll find that old people will become as dependent as you permit. The more chances they have to be on their own, the better. You seem to be doing well, Janet."

"I love it." And she did. Even apart from the great bonus of meeting Gerry, it was a satisfying way to spend her summer. Some money coming in and doing something worthwhile. As she moved toward full womanhood, Janet could feel the intensity of the urge to nurture and care for others. She could have been doing what Gerry did, mowing and the rest, but it was better to be working with the old people.

"Sometimes it almost seems like baby-sitting, Father."

"I know. But don't let on. If we live long enough, we seem to become again the children we were. Gerry is working out fine too."

But Gerry had to contend with Willy Fisk, the laziest man ever born, who took credit now for all the work Gerry did. At least Father Dowling wasn't fooled.

"Willy's had a very unfortunate life. It's his own fault, don't misunderstand. He tends to blame it on forces over which he had no control, but that's largely nonsense. His brother is a monsignor in Los Angeles, and they came from the same nest."

Janet wondered why Father Dowling rather than Monsignor Fisk had taken in the unfortunate Willy but thought better of asking. Father Dowling was a soft touch, that was clear, determined to see whatever good there might be in others but not really expecting much from someone like Willy Fisk.

"He calls it damage control," her mother said. "Maybe Willy won't get much better, but there's a chance he won't get worse."

"He'll get more rest with Gerry doing all the work."

Willy called his tours around the parish plant troubleshooting, which meant that he was looking for other jobs for Gerry to do. Of course, the important thing was to discover what had to be done, not to do it. He could retire to his apartment and play pinochle there with Mr. Walsh, sipping contraband beer as they did so.

"Willy has taken the pledge," her mother said sarcastically.

"The pledge?"

"He has vowed not to drink."

"But he drinks all the time."

"I know."

"Maybe he pledged to keep on drinking, not to stop."

Outside, the mower went by, drowning out whatever her mother replied. It was time to pick up her shoppers at the mall. It was two in the afternoon before she spoke to Gerry about the swimming party at Nick Stafford's.

"He's a kid in our class. They have a riverfront cottage, and we can swim right off their dock. My friend Beth, the one I told you about? She'll be there."

"Sure. Great. What time?"

It was that easy. She felt good about it for an hour, until she realized that what he had agreed to was a swimming party with other kids and that she had made it sound as if the main point was for him to meet Beth!

6

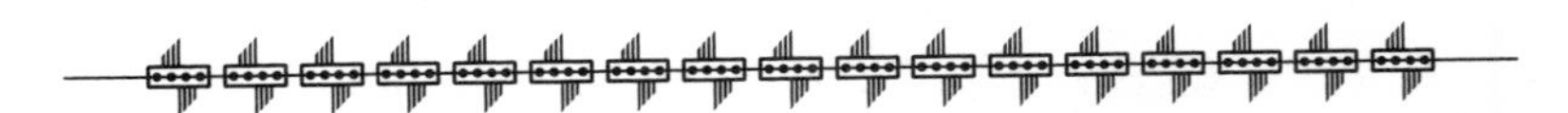

"So what has Patrick Crowe been up to since his release?" Father Dowling asked Phil Keegan. Gerry had gone off to a Cubs game with the ticket a parishioner had given the pastor. Father Dowling and Phil were happy enough to watch the game along with Steve Stone and Harry Caray.

"He's behaving like a choirboy. His parole officer got him a job with a rental-car agency—counter work, returning cars to the lot—and he has taken to it as if it were his life's ambition."

"So you're not worried."

"I wouldn't say that. Not that I would call it 'worry.' I just don't believe that those years at Joliet made an angel out of Patrick Crowe. He killed one man and all but got away with it, and if he could kill another on the same basis I'm not sure he wouldn't consider it a bargain."

Well, caution is a good thing, particularly in a policeman who makes enemies in the line of duty as a matter of course. Father Dowling did not find it hard to believe that Crowe might make an attempt on Phil Keegan's life. He had long since stopped being surprised by what humans are capable of, and not just those who have already done what Patrick Crowe had done. There had been a first time for him, and there could be a first time for anyone. On those occasions when Father Dowling had been quicker than Phil in seeing to the bottom of some crime it was because the priest could imagine himself in the plight of the poor devil who had robbed or killed or betrayed.

"Anyone is capable of anything, Phil, in certain conditions."

"That's a fine theory for a priest."

"Any other theory would be heresy."

Even so, he might have put thoughts of Crowe out of his mind if Willy Fisk hadn't come to him and told him about the stranger who had stopped Gerry Krause and asked about him.

"The way Gerry described him, Father, it had to be Patrick Crowe."

"Is he a friend of yours?"

"Friend?" Fisk turned away as if he intended to spit upon the floor, but he restrained himself. "A man like Crowe has no friends, he has people who owe him and others he owes. He always get paid and he never fails to pay."

"Do you owe him anything?"

"I'm not sure."

"Tell me about it."

Fisk had gone back to Joliet to visit a man who was his friend and in the course of the visit had told of his job at St. Hilary's. "I told him what good friends you and Captain Keegan are, Father."

"That's true."

"It was common knowledge that Patrick Crowe had promised to make anyone responsible for his conviction pay. Keegan was the cop who got the goods on him."

"But what has that to do with you? Did you know Crowe in prison?"

Fisk shook his head, and his narrow face was worried

under the sweatband he always wore as if it were a sign of the heavy labor in which he engaged.

"I was there, Father." He meant in prison. "He'll think that gives him a claim on me."

Father Dowling thanked the maintenance man for telling him about his worries. "Let me know immediately if he gets in touch with you."

"He said he'd surprise me."

"Would you like to change quarters?"

"Where would I go?"

Father Dowling had Edna Hospers fix up a room on the third floor of the school in what had once been the nurse's office. The change was to be kept secret. At least Fisk wouldn't be surprised in his bed.

"Why do you visit Joliet, Willy?"

"It got to be like a home to me, Father."

"How long were you in?"

"Which time?"

Phil Keegan, who had approved Father Dowling's hiring of Willy Fisk, saw the little man as basically harmless.

"Some people fail even at failure, Roger. Willy was lucky enough to never make it into the big time as a criminal."

Keegan also dismissed the visit to St. Hilary's by Patrick Crowe. "They're like kids, Father. He probably wanted to show off his new suit and shoes and take Willy for a spin in the company car."

Fisk might have made friends with the people his age who spent their day at the center, but he was content to keep aloof, except from Timothy Walsh.

"He keeps my books for me, Father."

"Books?"

"I'm a dry gambler."

Fisk's hobby was to study the sports pages daily and to

place hypothetical bets. He had started with an imaginary thousand and dutifully recorded his bets, his wins and losses.

"Tim has put a system into it with that laptop computer of his. He can call up any bet I've made, tell me just like that how I stand."

"How do you stand?"

Fisk fished a slip of paper from the pocket of his shirt and squinted at it. "I am seventy-five thousand, three hundred dollars to the good as of this morning. It will be more or less tomorrow."

"I should think you'd be tempted to bet for real."

Fisk shook his head. "I'd lose."

"Not if you made seventy-five thousand and stopped."

"That isn't the way it works. I was above a hundred once and within a week I was in the hole. You can't stop when your luck is good and you can't stop when it goes bad."

"Well, I admire your good sense."

The laptop computer Tim Walsh carried in his shoulder bag was the smallest Father Dowling had ever seen. Walsh was delighted to show it to him.

"Not much more than two pounds, Father, and it's powerful. The hard drive accommodates a tremendous amount of storage. I wish I'd had one of these when I started out."

"You were an accountant, weren't you?"

"Still am. Oh, I'm retired, but you don't spend a lifetime keeping track of things and just stop."

"Is Willy doing as well on his imaginary betting as he says?"

"What does he say?"

"That he has won over seventy thousand dollars."

Walsh smiled. "My wife, rest her soul, always finished the crossword puzzle. Every day, not a square left empty. She amazed her friends. Of course, she didn't tell them she did them a day late, when she had the answers too."

"What are you saying?"

"Willy bets on yesterday's races."

"Then he should never lose."

"If he didn't, I would suspect him."

"He doesn't know you know?"

"I'm telling you this in confidence, Father. He has to provide himself some bad luck so the good luck will stand out."

Patrick Crowe was unlikely to find work again in anything connected with the electronics industry, but news of his release from prison was carried in a trade paper that Phil Keegan showed to Father Dowling. The article detailed the way in which Crowe had kept himself informed of the inventories of local warehouses and then hired professionals to break in and steal. There was a note of grudging admiration in the article. The precautions that had been introduced as a result of Crowe's thefts were hinted at rather than described.

"There's something for his scrapbook," Phil said with disgust.

"There's no mention of the man who was killed."

"Ah, you noticed. What's a mere murder when you have such a crafty scheme to write about?"

Gerry Krause studied the photograph of Patrick Crowe that accompanied the story. It showed the man on his way into court, flanked by his lawyers, glancing at the camera.

"Of course he's younger there than when you saw him, Gerry. *If* you saw him, that is."

"Oh, this is the man. He doesn't look much older now."

"Let's hope he's wiser."

"Can I show this to Willy Fisk, Father Dowling?"

"Maybe he's jumpy enough as it is."

"I'd want to see it if I were him."

"Would you? I suppose you're right. Sure, take it along
don't think Phil wants it."

Phil and Cy Horvath seemed as interested as Fisk might be in keeping an eye on Patrick Crowe and seeing how he was settling into civilian life.

"I told you, Roger, he's a choirboy. Always arrives at work on time, spends eight hours at the dullest job God ever created, and does it with a smile on his face. They can't keep kids just out of high school behind those counters for much more than a month, it's so boring. We'll see how long he lasts."

Gerry and Janet talked over the strange visit of Patrick Crowe to St. Hilary's several times. The fact that it seemed wise to relocate Willy Fisk on the third floor of the school, where he could sleep more safely than in his apartment in the basement, made it obvious that Father Dowling at least was willing to take Fisk's jumpiness seriously.

"Maybe he just meant a surprise visit," Janet said.

"Maybe. The way he said it, though, it sounded more like a threat. Apparently he threatened my uncle at the time he was convicted."

Gerry told her the story as he had learned it from his Uncle Phil. Janet listened with a solemn expression on her face.

"It was your uncle who arrested my father, Gerry. My mother still half blames him for what happened. That doesn't make much sense, but I understand it."

Gerry, caught up on his yardwork, came along when she took a minibus full of oldsters to the airport and a tour of the air-traffic control center. That was when Gerry had the idea that they ought to check out Crowe at work. The rental car counters were all in a row on the lower level, near the baggage pickup. Patrick Crowe stood out among the youthful people behind the counters; besides, he was the only male.

He looked flamboyant in his red jacket and black bow tie, and he had the knack of talking while he was smiling.

"He looks harmless enough," Janet said.

"He can't be earning much more money than we do."

They were on the far side of a baggage carousel, which was disgorging luggage as passengers jostled to get in closer. Gerry doubted that Crowe would recognize him, but the idea was to watch without being watched. The alternative was to just march up to the counter, where he could remind Crowe of their first meeting and ask when he planned to surprise Willy Fisk. For all they were finding out standing here watching Crowe supply customers with rental cars, they might have done that. Janet was struck by the comment about how little Crowe's job paid.

"Where does he live?"

"I checked into that. He's staying at a halfway house for people just out of prison. Apparently there's next to no charge for that, although he can't stay there forever."

"Who told you that, your uncle?"

"No. There's no need to tell him I'm trying to put Willy Fisk's mind at ease. Do you know Lieutenant Cy Horvath?"

"I know who he is."

"I talked to him. Made it sound just like curiosity. That's all it is anyway, I suppose. Looking after Willy seems to be my job, and if I can put his mind at ease I will."

"I thought you said Crowe's remark sounded like a threat."

"It did."

That made what they were doing more than a way to pass time while Janet's charges were being told about air-traffic control. Gerry would have liked to hear about that himself, but Janet told him they could do that on their own on another occasion, and he agreed. It wasn't that he found the old people a nuisance, but it would be more fun with just Janet. He found he was looking forward to the swimming party coming up that weekend.

When they arrived back at the school there was some commotion. Walsh and Willy Fisk were in Mrs. Hospers's office, and Father Dowling had just arrived from the house. Walsh's laptop computer was missing, and he was very upset.

"Where did you last see it?"

"Father, I carry it around in a shoulder bag, and I almost never let that bag out of my sight. It's not that I distrust people, it's just habit. Besides, it's valuable—not just in itself but to me. All my data is in it."

"Do you have backup copies?"

"Some. Yes." But Walsh's expression made it clear that a few disks full of data could hardly make up for the loss of his computer. "The only place I ever put it down was in Willy's place. That's where I must have left it before I got into the game of shuffleboard with Agatha Young."

Agatha was interviewed, and with a near-sighted blue-eyed smile she thought about the question and then said she honestly couldn't remember. "You always have that bag slung over your shoulder, Tim. I can almost see it now."

"I couldn't very well play shuffleboard with that hanging on my shoulder."

Agatha reacted as if she thought that it was herself rather than his bag that Timothy Walsh spoke of so disdainfully as hanging from his shoulder. Agatha was notorious for developing crushes on the eligible men—meaning widowers—who came to the center. Walsh with his white hair and white mustache and unwrinkled skin that seemed to wear a permanent tan was a favorite in any case, and Agatha had been glad to lure him away as her partner in shuffleboard.

"Partner?" Father Dowling asked. "Who was the opposing team?"

The Waterses, a couple in their midseventies who were inseparable and had been for fifty years. There were no Waters children, and Mrs. Waters had worked at her husband's side in the pharmacy that had been their life as well as their livelihood. They consulted one another and agreed that Tim Walsh had not been wearing his shoulder bag when he played shuffleboard.

"It would get in the way," Mrs. Waters said.

"It would impede the free swing of the arm," Mr. Waters said. He illustrated what he meant, as far as his arthritis would allow.

Others drew near while this inquiry went on, and soon there was a general though unorganized search going on, with chairs being moved, tables looked under, reminiscences exchanged.

"I saw Tim first thing this morning."

"Did he have it with him then?"

"His bag? I think he did."

"The computer was in the bag."

"I didn't see that."

"Of course you didn't see it."

"Oh, Tim showed it to me once. Proud as punch of the thing. Looked like a glorified calculator to me."

"What do you know about computers?"

"Only what Tim told me. Did he ever show the thing to you?"

Janet smiled at Gerry, who beckoned Willy Fisk over. "Have you searched your apartment for the bag, Willy?"

"If it's there it would be obvious. It's not as big as a breadbox, but you could hardly hide the thing."

"Janet and I will look around, okay?"

Fisk threw up his hands. "Feel free. I've got no rights. Someone loses his damned computer and I'm treated like a suspect. I might just as well be back in you know where."

Fisk unlocked the door to his apartment and stood aside for them to go in.

"Do you always keep the door locked?" Janet asked him.

"Not when I'm inside. Except at night, of course." He whispered, "When I sleep here, I mean."

It was still a secret where Willy Fisk's bed was now. The apartment seemed unusually neat, perhaps because Fisk now used it only during the day and didn't spend much time there. The thought of a surprise visit from Patrick Crowe kept him moving around among the old people, kibitzing at cards, flirting with the ladies, out where he could be seen. It was a wonder Agatha hadn't snared him as her partner in shuffleboard.

Fisk left them alone, but even so it seemed odd to be rummaging around among his things. The shoulder bag was certainly not in plain sight. The closet, when opened, seemed almost empty. Apparently Fisk had transferred his clothing to the third floor. Not that he seemed to have much. His jeans and T-shirt and headband were a uniform, the only variation being in foot gear. Sometimes he wore white gym shoes, sometimes black loafers with a high shine and leather heels that clicked authoritatively down the hallway of the school. In the kitchen, Janet opened the broom closet and looked in. She turned to Gerry.

"It certainly isn't here."

Gerry agreed. When they came back into the recreation room, Timothy Walsh was being urged to retrace his steps since he had risen that morning—physically, and not just in his mind.

"Go home and reenact the whole thing," Agatha said with

uncustomary enthusiasm. "It's what I do, and it always works."

"You could pray to St. Anthony," someone said. "He never fails."

"Oh, I do that too," Agatha said.

There were murmurs of agreement and several began testimonials to the aid of the saint in finding lost articles.

"I know I had it with me," Walsh protested.

"Timothy, you have lost it, so don't act as if you've never made a mistake. Chances are you'll find it at home."

"I never go out without that shoulder bag. You all know that."

Eventually he was prevailed upon to do what Agatha said. She offered to accompany him and this was seconded all around, not without some giggling and snickering. The two of them got into the minibus and Janet drove away with them, her head cocked as she listened to the directions Timothy Walsh was giving her.

8

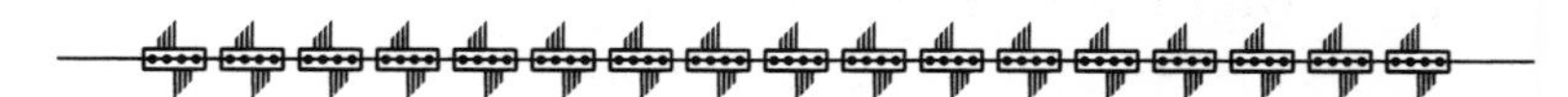

Edna Hospers got away from the commotion while Tim Walsh was still receiving unsolicited advice in the recreation room and went back to her office. Walsh had offered to help her with her paperwork and any accounting she might have, but she had put him off, not only because Father Dowling's lawyer took care of most of what she assumed Mr. Walsh had in mind but also because she was jealous of her domain.

When Father Dowling, faced with an empty and deteriorating school, conceived the idea of a parish center that might do some good for his aging parishioners—the young had moved to the suburbs, leaving their parents in St. Hilary's, and the need of the school had passed—he had asked Edna to take charge. She had never done such a thing in her life before, and she more than half suspected that he had made the offer to help her through the bad time after what had happened to Earl. Her first reaction was to refuse.

"I wouldn't know where to start, Father Dowling."

"Start small and see what happens."

There had been an announcement in the parish bulletin informing those interested that the school would be open on weekday mornings for those who wished to get together there. Mrs. Edna Hospers would be the director of the St. Hilary's parish center. The difference between that grandiose title and the reality of those first weeks was almost total, but Edna found that the old people who came did not expect everything to be done for them. They wanted to be in on the planning, so that is what they did at first. In between card games, they talked about what the center might become. Father Dowling responded to every reasonable suggestion. Many who came had experience of other centers for the retired and what was provided there, so they had that to go on. Within a year the operation could be referred to as the St. Hilary's parish center without irony.

For Edna it had been a godsend. Not only did it provide her with an essential income to support the family she had been left alone with, but it took her mind off her troubles. She was not a woman given to self-pity, but she would have had to be Superwoman not to feel sorry for herself after what had happened—suddenly, it seemed—to her marriage and family. One day she'd had a husband to care for her and the children, to provide them with shelter and clothing and food; and the next her husband was gone and she was alone. Not only was he gone, he was engulfed in shame and notoriety. Edna learned to keep up her chin as she stayed at his side during his ordeal, and after the sentence was read, when they were saying goodbye before he was taken away, she surprised herself with the courage she showed.

"Nothing can destroy our marriage," she promised. "I love you."

The expression on his face as he heard these words burned itself into her heart. It was as if she was his one remaining claim to membership in the human family. She was resolved not to abandon him. She did not permit the children to forget him. He had done wrong—there was no doubt about that, terrible wrong—and now he was paying for it. But one day his debt would be paid and he would come home and they would welcome him back with open arms. Thus far she had respected his wish that none of the children should see him as a prisoner.

"I couldn't bear it, Edna. I couldn't. I try to imagine my own dad here and I can't."

It was the kids he wanted to protect as much as himself. Edna had to bear along with him the ignominy of the supervised visits, the coldness of the guards and prison officials, the shame that would not go away. But they bore it together, and that made it almost bearable.

Next to detailed accounts of family life and of the kids, Earl liked to hear all about her job and what was going on at the parish center. So of course she had told him when Willy Fisk was hired by Father Dowling.

"Willy!" Earl made a face.

"Do you know him?"

He shook his head. It was clear that Willy was the kind of fellow prisoner he had no wish to know. Not that Willy was one of the truly bad ones.

"He's a nickel-and-dimer, Edna. I hope Father Dowling knows what he's doing."

"You might mention it to him."

"Oh, I wouldn't want to spoil things for Willy. Anyway, he's harmless, in his way."

In his way. Fisk was a petty thief who had been caught almost as often as he stole, who had spent time in lesser institutions until the sheer repetition of his thievery had sent him to Joliet.

"That cured me," he said to Edna. They never mentioned Earl, but Edna was sure Fisk spoke so freely to her because of Earl. "In a city or county jail, you see more bad luck than bad character. But in Joliet, you're in the big leagues. I don't want to play that kind of ball and I have no intention of going back."

If Fisk had no intention of committing some terrible crime for which he could be sent back to Joliet, he clearly did not mean to be everything he should be. He had accepted the offer of a job from Father Dowling and expended more energy avoiding work than he ever devoted to it. Edna did not frame the thought, but she was no doubt struck by her own very different response to the opportunity the priest had offered her. Willy Fisk was lazy, and he told tall tales to anyone foolish enough to listen. Edna, who knew his story, was amazed by the elaborate accounts he gave others as to how he had spent his life: war hero, intrepid construction worker in far-flung countries, veteran of the seas, and athlete, of course. That he might have made a living playing professional ball or golf was an assumption of his stories. Edna could kick herself for listening to such drivel, but she had to admit he told a great tale. Is that how he had spent his time in prison, living imaginary lives?

In the end, Edna was not amused. However funny it might seem that the folks who came to the parish center—people who had worked all their lives, raised children, known hardship as well as success—should give credence to the fabulous stories of a rascal like Willy Fisk did not seem at all funny when Edna told herself that Fisk was probably deceiving her too in ways she didn't even suspect. Such thoughts settled on her mind when Tim Walsh's shoulder bag and computer were missing.

She rose from her desk, left her office, and went down the long hallway as if in a trance, trying not to think of what she was doing. The stairway she took to the third floor was not one on which she was likely to meet any of her charges. The old people sometimes wandered about the school, especially those who had attended it as children, stirring up nostalgia or perhaps not. On the third floor, she went rapidly to the door of the former nurse's office, where she hesitated. She turned and glanced back at the stairway up which she had come; she looked up and down the corridor of the third floor. Then she turned the knob and eased the door open. She was not surprised to find it unlocked. She did not turn on the light. The window blinds were tipped to admit enough light. Fisk's bed was unmade, of course. A portable television stood on a chair at the foot of his bed. A bowl sat on the floor beside the bed with a few unpopped kernels in it. The shoulder bag was in the closet. She opened it to make sure the computer was inside. Her first thought was that it was stupid of Fisk not to have locked his door, but of course she had a master key for the school and could have let herself in. But no one else could have. No doubt he hadn't realized what a fuss Timothy Walsh would raise when he realized his computer was gone.

She put the bag back into the closet, and when she left the room she locked the door behind her. Although she walked rapidly to the stairway, she descended slowly, unsure of what to do. By the time she passed the second landing she knew. This was something for Father Dowling to handle.

9

When Tim Walsh and that yo-yo Agatha were driven away by Edna Hospers's daughter, Willy Fisk felt the pressure was off. How much was that computer worth anyway? Walsh acted as if the crown jewels were missing and the whole place had to come to a standstill until his stupid shoulder bag was found. He did look undressed without it, Fisk gave him that. The guy toted the bag around as if he were a mailman on his rounds. Handy when he got it out and figured up Fisk's wins and losses, though. Did he even suspect that Fisk placed his bets on the evening of the day the races were run? Naw. He wouldn't enter into the bookkeeping with such relish if he knew Fisk were just pretending in several ways—imaginary money but imaginary risks as well. Fisk's idea of the good life was to have the gift to know in advance how every game and race played or run that day would come out. Not guessing, not calculating, but knowing. With that kind of knowledge you could rule the world.

"That's the kind of knowledge God has," Father Dowling had observed when Fisk told him this.

"Well, He rules the world, doesn't He?"

It was odd to think of God as a gambler who knew everything and in that way had an advantage over everyone else. But what did he have to win?

Fisk hadn't pursued the topic. He had learned how dangerous it could be to get into conversations like that with a padre. Over the years, he had been the object of any number of efforts to convert him, to get him to change his life, efforts especially by his brother, the monsignor. Most of the arguments made it sound like the smart thing to do. Be good and be a winner. Sure, look at Jesus. Another remark he wasn't likely to make to Father Dowling.

At first he had felt contempt for the priest, who'd hired him when he knew so little about him. Dowling had seemed like just another man of the cloth who had made up his mind to ignore the facts and pretend things and people were different than they were. But gradually Fisk realized that he wasn't fooling Dowling at all. It was as if the priest hadn't really expected to get any work out of him. And then he hired Gerry. Fisk took full advantage of that, but he was beginning to have the feeling that the joke was on him. He sensed what Edna Hospers thought of him, and as for Marie Murkin the housekeeper, forget it. If she had her way, Willy Fisk would have been given the bums's rush out of St. Hilary's months ago. But even the old people had started to treat him as a bit of a joke, including Timothy Walsh.

The shoulder bag had suddenly turned all eyes on him, as if he had taken the damned thing. What was he supposed to do with a computer? "Sell it," a voice within him said, and despite himself he wondered what it would bring. He'd like to find the bag himself and then hide it. Walsh had already lost his computer—that was his fault—so finding it and not telling wouldn't really change anything. Maybe he could find a fence who'd take a computer and make a little money.

He shuffled down the hall toward the stairway, and when he heard footsteps coming down, went into a classroom. A moment later Edna Hospers went past, moving right along.

Fisk waited, then went on to the stairs and started up to his hideaway. He wanted to just get out of the way and lie low for a while. No doubt Janet would soon bring Walsh back, and the man would have his bag slung over his shoulder and the whole thing would be over with. In the meantime, Willy would take a little nap.

The door of the nurse's office was locked, and that puzzled him. He only locked it at night when he came up here to sleep, to get out of harm's way in case Patrick Crowe had any strange ideas. It was unhealthy for both of them to have the names of Willy Fisk and Patrick Crowe connected.

He unlocked the door, let himself in, then locked the door behind him. He stood there, eyes closed, and had the feeling that he wasn't alone. He sniffed. There was some kind of smell: perfume, a woman's smell. Of course. That was the scent Edna Hospers wore. He was sure of it. So she had been up here. She must have locked the door, but why? Standing still, he looked around the room. The blades of the window blind threw bars of sunlight and shadow across the floor, across his bed, against the wall. The bed looked the way he had left it, and the television, and the bowl from which he had eaten popcorn while he watched the tube the night before. Slowly he moved across the room, drawn to the closet. He opened the door slowly and fell back when he saw the shoulder bag.

His first thought was to get out of there, fast, to get downstairs and mingle with the others, to see and be seen, but he stood frozen, looking at the shoulder bag. His second thought made more sense. He took the bag, slung it over his shoulder, sauntered out of the room, and started downstairs, making as much noise as he could. When he came into the first-floor corridor, he let out a shout.

"I found it! Everybody relax! I found Walsh's computer."

Edna Hospers came to the door of her office, and Fisk gave her a withering look. She had tried to frame him and it hadn't worked. All the days he had been worrying about Patrick Crowe playing a practical joke on him—or worse—and the real danger had been right at his elbow.

"You got Tim's home number, you might give him a call, Edna. Put his mind at rest, know what I mean?"

He went past her into her office, eased the bag from his shoulder, and put it on her desk. Grinning, he went into the hallway, where he tried to whistle; but his lips couldn't keep from smiling and that ruined it.

10

Edna called and asked Father Dowling if he could come over to the school please, it was about the missing computer.

"Tim find it at home?"

"No. I'd rather tell you here, Father."

Edna was not given to odd requests, so he went over, but when he got there she seemed less sure of herself than she had on the phone. The shoulder bag lay on the desk. Father Dowling unzipped it and looked at the computer. It seemed intact.

"Where did you find it?"

She closed the hall door and sat down behind her desk and told him a very strange story. On impulse she had checked the room on the third floor in which Willy Fisk had been sleeping since the strange visit of Patrick Crowe, and there she had found the computer in the closet.

"And you brought it down?" asked Father Dowling.

"No, *he* did. Bold as brass. When I found it in his closet I decided I'd leave it there, call you, and see what you thought ought to be done. As soon as I hung up, Willy came down the hall, yelling that he had found the bag. He came in and put it there. Father, the way he looked at me, he knew I'd found it."

"What do you think I ought to do?"

"I don't know. Now that he's returned it . . ."

"I don't know either. For the moment, why don't we just let it go?"

She didn't like the suggestion. Father Dowling didn't much like it himself. The trouble was that there were too many interpretations of what Edna had told him. The most obvious possibility was that Fisk had cast himself in the role of minor hero, the man who could find the valuable missing bag when everyone else had given up. His arrival, as Edna described it, fit that theory. On the other hand, there was the possibility that he had intended to steal the computer, saw that its absence had created too much of a fuss, and decided to "find" it instead and come downstairs with the big announcement.

Janet returned with Tim Walsh and Agatha, and the good news was cried out to them. Fisk came into Edna's office, picked up the shoulder bag, and went out to greet Walsh. Father Dowling followed him out. It seemed a bad way to end his conversation with Edna, but then another possible explanation had occurred to him. A few minutes later, as they paced on the sidewalk that ran between the school and the rectory, Fisk put it into words.

"She tried to frame me, Father. She put that bag in the room upstairs where I've been sleeping, and I suppose she was going to lead a search party up there, and where would I have been?"

"She called me to say she had found it upstairs, Willy."

"She called you!"

"That's right."

Fisk shook his head as if the international record for the unbelievable had just been broken.

"I know she doesn't like me, but why would she do something like this? Doesn't she know what another conviction could mean for me?"

"Why do you say she doesn't like you?"

"She doesn't." Fisk spoke with the sad certainty of a man more familiar with being disliked than liked. "What are you going to do about it, Father?"

"I'm not sure. Do you have any suggestions?"

"You have to talk with her."

"I'll certainly talk with her. Look, Willy, I've been given two versions of events; one by you, another by Edna. Chances are, that's the way it would end up no matter what I did, your word against hers, and vice versa."

"I didn't steal that bag, Father."

If that was true, he could hardly expect Fisk to see the wisdom of just putting the episode behind them.

"Willy, I can believe you and I can believe Edna as well. She found the bag in that room on the third floor, yet neither she nor you put it there. Who else might have done that?"

It was what, in Father Dowling's youth, was called the sixty-four-dollar question. Before Fisk could dismiss the possibility as a distraction something occurred to him and he stopped. He squinted at Father Dowling, then looked over his shoulder at the school.

"Crowe," he whispered. "Patrick Crowe. This must be the surprise he promised me."

"But why would he do that to you?"

Fisk shrugged. It was obvious that he was losing interest in the subject. "You'd have to know him to understand."

"Why does he have a grudge against you? I thought you didn't really know him."

"Who says he has a grudge against me?"

"This wasn't a very funny joke."

"Maybe it wasn't Crowe. That's just a guess, Father. The more I think of it, I'm sure it had to be Edna. But you're right: Why make a federal case out of it? Let bygones be bygones, I say."

Up the walk toward them came Timothy Walsh. The familiar bag was slung over his shoulder, and there was a grateful smile on his face.

"Willy, let me buy you a beer. I can't tell you what a relief it is to get my computer back." He put his hand on Fisk's shoulder and looked at Father Dowling. "I'm ashamed to say it, but I had even begun to wonder if Willy here hadn't taken the thing. As a joke."

"Maybe I did," Fisk said with a grin. "Maybe I did."

The two men went back to the school together, arm in arm, and Father Dowling stood looking at them go. It would have been hard to say which was the odder of those two, Tim Walsh or Willy Fisk. Did the accountant know that the man with whom he was walking arm in arm had spent a significant portion of his life behind bars? Perhaps it did not matter now as once it would have, when Walsh was active in his profession. Age and the parish center at St. Hilary's put everything into a different perspective.

"Could it have been Crowe?" he asked Phil Keegan that evening. Phil had no objection to talking about such matters with Gerry in the room, and Father Dowling himself saw no reason that the boy shouldn't take part.

"It could have been anyone. Gerry might have stashed the bag in the man's closet. If anyone other than he himself did, that is. I'm inclined to take the simplest explanation, the one Edna gave. Depend upon it, she's had enough chance to observe that bird to sense what he might or might not do. If she thinks he did it, I'm inclined to believe her."

"And when did you begin to put such trust in feminine

intuition, Captain Keegan?" Marie Murkin stood in the door of the kitchen, smoothing her apron, a brow arched as she looked at the pastor's guest.

"Who said anything about feminine intuition? I mean exactly the opposite. I'm saying that Edna has had enough *experience* of the man to read his character aright."

"Then when did you give women credit for learning from experience?"

"Women? Who's talking about women? I'm talking about Edna Hospers and Edna Hospers alone. I have known this woman and that woman, but I have never known the composite creature to whom you refer, Marie Murkin."

"I won't argue with you," Marie said helplessly.

"Is that what you're doing? I wondered what it was."

Father Dowling came to his housekeeper's rescue. Keegan and Marie were ever engaged in uneven battle. Sometimes she had the advantage, sometimes he did; today things were definitely going Keegan's way. But Marie brushed away his attempt to help her.

"Listen to Willy Fisk is my advice. Why is he sleeping where he is now, up on the third floor of the school, if we didn't believe him before? If he could be believed then he can be believed now, and you had best look into the whereabouts of Mr. Patrick Crowe, Captain Philip Keegan."

Marie turned grandly on her heels and went into her kitchen, letting the door between swing to and fro in a diminishing arc, making a hushing sound as it did so.

"What do you say, Gerry?"

"Father, I'm just glad Mr. Walsh got his computer back."

11

The swimming party at the Stafford cottage on the banks of the Fox River went well. Gerry had wondered if accepting Janet's invitation meant they were going together—on a date—or they were just there with a bunch of other kids for the sake of the swimming and the picnic. But his main concern had been meeting a bunch of new kids all at once. Luckily that had turned out to be no big deal and everything had gone well. Swimmingly, as he would later tell Mrs. Murkin. Janet's friend Beth was kind of weird, but then he had been more or less prepared for that, as much by what Janet didn't say as by what she did.

"Do you see a lot of Janet during the day or what?" Beth asked him. "I mean, if you're mowing and working on the grounds and she's inside taking care of all those old people, when do you see one another?"

"Janet who?"

Beth's mouth fell open and she stared at him a moment before she decided he was kidding. "Gerry, I'm serious. Tell me what you do all day."

"Did you ever cut grass?"

"Well, I've trimmed a little."

"The thing about grass, it's pretty much all alike. Clover's different. Once in a while you'll find a four-leaf clover, but one blade of grass is exactly like another."

Janet came to the rescue, bringing one of the first hamburgers from the grill. Beth wandered away as if in search of some boy she could serve. He seemed to be making the impression on Beth that Janet hoped he would. It wasn't the first time he felt they were a team. Father Dowling had given them the minibus for the occasion, and later, when he drove her home if not before, he intended to talk with her about the conversation his uncle and Father Dowling had had about Mr. Walsh's shoulder bag and computer.

Now that they had started eating, the swimming was over. Gerry was used to swimming in lakes, but he found the Fox River required somewhat different skills. Janet dove from the dock and swam straight as an arrow out into the river for twenty yards before she turned to look back where she had come. When she started toward the shore again, she did so at an angle, to overcome the current of the river. Gerry had the sense that she was letting him know how the river was without telling him, and he appreciated it. He noticed the way the kids kept an eye on each other too, one staying by the dock while another struck out into the river, waiting for the other to return.

"The buddy system," Janet said. She did not have to add that they were buddies.

There were three guys and three girls; one of the girls was, like Nick, on the cheerleading squad. While the two of them went onto the small lawn in front of the cottage to get in a little gymnastic exercise, the Stafford canoe was at the disposal of the others. Gerry, however, claimed a flat-bottomed boat that looked as if it could have gone through the Flood without mishap, and he rowed Janet slowly upriver. The idea was that he would wear himself out going against the current and then let it take them effortlessly back to the cottage.

"Willy told Father Dowling that your mother planted Walsh's computer in that room on the third floor in order to get him in trouble."

"As if he needs help. That's what Mom figured he would do."

"There's another possibility."

"Sure, what happened: He stole it."

"Okay, a third possibility. What if Crowe did it?"

"Crowe!"

Gerry developed the idea and could see that she was beginning to find it plausible. She sat at the end of the boat, wearing a terry-cloth robe she had slipped on before getting into the boat. Her legs were stretched out in front of her, and she wriggled her toes as she thought. In a bathing suit, with these kids, now in the boat, Janet seemed almost a different person. The same, but more interesting. If he had first seen her like this Gerry doubted he could have become friends with her so easily. He laid into the rowing, fixing his eyes on a point upriver beyond her, conscious that he was showing off for her.

"Gerry, someone would have seen him."

"If someone had, it wouldn't have been a secret. Janet, I told him Willy worked in the school. Anyone can walk into the school during the day and wander anywhere they like."

"But he wouldn't have known about the room on the third floor."

"That's true."

He felt deflated. He should have thought of that. Father Dowling or his uncle should have thought of that when they'd discussed it in the pastor's study.

"Unless Willy told him," Janet added.

"What do you mean?"

She had let one hand hang over the side and was staring at the water as it moved through her fingers. She was thinking. Her eyes were bright when she looked at him.

"Maybe that's the joke. The two of them are in it together. Willy and Crowe." She sat up, pulling her robe together as she leaned toward him. "Sure, it's kids' stuff. Fool the grownups. But isn't that the way they are? You know Willy a lot better than I do, or want to, and you yourself have said he acts like some kid on the playground in grade school."

"But what's the point?"

"Attention! All eyes on Willy Fisk. A big commotion while the bag is searched for, he lets me drive Mr. Walsh all the way home on a wild goose chase, maybe he even expected that the others would begin to think he had done it, turn on him, accuse him. And then—voilà, the big revelation, reprieve, acclaim."

Gerry laughed and let up on the oars. "You ought to be a writer."

"Maybe I will be. Gerry, that's the way it could have happened. Then the room is no problem. In fact, that makes it better. Remember Willy has that hideaway bedroom because he's supposed to be afraid of Crowe. What do you think?"

"Nothing is impossible," he said, swinging the boat around and shipping the oars.

"To the Lord. You sound like Father Dowling. You ought to be a priest."

"Maybe I will be."

Her mouth opened. Before he could assure her he was kidding, the boat began to turn in the tide and he had to get the oars into the water and direct it. When he had it under control she was still peering at him, now with the corners of her mouth moving as if unsure whether to smile or not.

"Sure I think it could have happened that way. Willy is kid enough to do something like that."

"Of course, it's just wild speculation."

She pulled in her legs and tugged the belt of the robe more tightly around her middle. Her hair was thoroughly dry now after swimming, and it began to billow a bit in the breeze.

"Well, speculation. But why else did we check out Crowe at his airport counter if we weren't curious about the guy? Maybe we ought to be more systematic about it."

"What do you mean?"

"Do what Uncle Phil or Cy Horvath would do. Keep an eye on him."

"At work?"

"There's not much point in that; besides, we don't have the time during the day. I mean in the evening, check him out where he lives, see what he does, who his friends are. He doesn't have much freedom of movement—at least he isn't supposed to, living in a halfway house—but I doubt that he would worry too much about rules. And the way my uncle talks, any rules there are wouldn't be applied too strictly. Of course, he thinks all criminals are coddled."

"*Coddled:* What does that mean?"

"You're the writer, look it up."

"Yes, Father."

But when their eyes met he saw that, whatever chances she might have of becoming a writer, there was no likelihood at all that he was destined for the seminary.

"Want me to row awhile?"

"Sure. The next time we go upstream."

He bumped into the dock. She hopped out and secured the boat, then he followed her up the steps to where the others awaited them.

12

Marie was glad to see Gerry taking an interest in Janet, even if the girl was Edna Hospers's daughter. She had wondered if spending the summer in a rectory room meant for an assistant pastor would set his mind going on a possible vocation. That was always a danger, and the more so with a priest like Roger Dowling, who had his head on straight and lived a life any boy could imagine himself living. When the three of them got together in the study with the television blasting out some game or other, Marie sat at the kitchen table sipping tea and shaking her head. Men never did grow up completely, she knew that. After all, she had married one who'd scarcely grown up at all and may God have mercy on his soul. All that camaraderie surely made staying in the house a pleasant thing for the boy, as Phil Keegan had had the good sense to see. It was the difficulty getting back and forth to the parish from Phil Keegan's apartment that had decided him in favor of Gerry's staying here with Father Dowling. Marie had seen no dangerous signs of ostentatious piety, no assumption that he was expected to go to Mass every day or act as if he really were something like an assistant pastor, and now the way Gerry and Janet got along was more reassurance.

But now that she felt she need no longer worry about Gerry daydreaming himself into a seminary, she began to worry that he might get too serious about Janet. The alternative to the seminary wasn't tying himself down to one girl, not at the age of sixteen, certainly.

"He ought to meet more people his own age," she suggested to the pastor one morning when Gerry set out across the yard to the maintenance shed.

"There's Janet."

"That's true."

"What have you got against Janet?"

"Not a thing. She's a wonderful girl. But he's how old, sixteen? He probably would like to meet some boys his own age."

"He met some the other night when they went swimming in the river."

"A party. I meant just some other boys."

"He has Phil and me."

"Ha. Don't forget Willy Fisk; there's another fine male companion for him."

"You're just jealous."

"Of what? Of Willy Fisk! The famous lost-and-found department suddenly, isn't he?" Marie started to move toward the kitchen. "It's impossible having anything like a rational conversation with you anymore, Father Dowling."

"I'm sorry, Marie. Let's have a rational conversation."

She kept her eye fixed on him to make sure it wasn't one of his ironical remarks and then spoke. But it was Willy Fisk and the lost-and-found computer she talked of, somewhat to her own surprise. "What a great to-do about nothing, wasn't it, Father? Honestly, nearly every one of them was milling about as if the sky had fallen, looking for Tim Walsh's shoulder bag. How they love a fuss."

"You can hardly blame Tim Walsh for being concerned. I don't know what such a computer costs, but it would be a considerable amount, and then he has so much of his work stored on it."

"I don't understand a thing about it."

"He'd be happy to explain it to you. Now Marie, I don't mean anything. People who use computers have a bad habit of wanting to talk about little else. I myself received the fifty-drachma course the first time we talked."

"The what?"

"Something from Plato. It doesn't matter. So be careful what you say to Tim."

He was at it again but with a straight face, so there wasn't anything she could say. She went to her kitchen and got things ready for the lunch she would serve him when he returned from saying his noon Mass. He liked a cold lunch in the summer, so she made a salad with pasta left over from the night before and iced tea, though that was for herself. He drank nothing but coffee, morning, noon, and night and four seasons a year. The tea was for herself and Gerry. Having a growing boy at her table gave greater importance to preparing meals. She could have served the pastor buttered cardboard and a bowl of carpet tacks and he wouldn't have noticed. And then she thought it would be nice to have Janet for lunch too. There would be more than enough for everyone, given the way the pastor ate.

"Speak of the devil," she cried when she ran into Tim Walsh on the walk leading to the school. He looked over his shoulder, took her arm, and began to walk her back the way she had come.

"What's the matter?"

He smiled at her, enlisting her sympathy. "One *can* get too much of a good thing, Mrs. Murkin. You know Agatha, I suppose."

Father Dowling, cynic that he was, would have said that

Tim Walsh was taking the surest route to gain a woman's interest by criticizing another and expecting her to join in, but the theory didn't take account of women like Agatha who made pests of themselves and took advantage of cultivated old gentlemen like Tim Walsh. His complexion was pink, his hair snow white, and his well-groomed little mustache, when it spread in a smile, revealed a row of perfect teeth that, if they weren't Mother Nature's, nevertheless needed a keen eye to tell the difference. As usual, Tim Walsh was nattily attired, in green polo shirt, cream-colored slacks, and summer shoes with sensible soles. The hair on the arm that held her elbow was silvery against the skin.

"Agatha," Marie said.

"Do you play shuffleboard, Mrs. Murkin?"

She freed her elbow. Did he think she had nothing better to do than while away the day at the parish center like those old people?

"Of course you don't. Neither do I, except as an accommodation. Cards, now, I love cards."

"Bridge?"

"Do you play? But of course you would. Bridge is a game that engages the mind, not the muscles. I play duplicate once a week."

Marie's game was so-so, and the women she played with got together to exercise their mouths rather than their minds, but there was no need to disturb Timothy Walsh's notion that she was some kind of intellectual. Was he all that far off, when one stopped to think of it?

"How glad you must be to have your computer back," she said to him.

"You noticed I'm not carrying it."

She noticed it now. "I don't wonder you're more careful now."

"It is taking it off my shoulder that is careless, not keeping it on." He leaned toward her, taking her elbow again. "I have it locked in the trunk of my car. Which is parked in the shade."

"You drive here?" Most of the others were near enough to walk or were picked up by Janet in the minibus if walking was impractical and they weren't too far distant.

"I did today. For the first time. Because of my computer."

"I don't understand a thing about them."

"You understand them enough to know they don't walk off by themselves and hide themselves in closets."

"What a mystery."

"Do you think so?"

"Don't you?"

He worked his lips, making his mustache move. "No. Willy Fisk is of course the key."

"Of course."

"Of two things, one: Either he took my bag, hid it, and then produced it to great fanfare after everyone had been searching high and low for it."

"That sounds like Willy."

Tim Walsh held up his hand. "Or, two: Someone is playing a trick on him, or tried to, and he managed to foil it. Imagine if the bag had been discovered in that room and he faced the task of explaining how it got there. Who would have believed him?"

"So which do you prefer?"

"The second. The first strikes you as being in character for Willy, and you may be right. But it fails to take into account an important factor. Even before this contretemps, Willy and I had become friends. It would be too much to expect him to play bridge or, if he did, to get two others of sufficient skill to make it interesting, but he can play pinochle."

"Does that take brains?"

"Very little. But it requires that the opponent be moderately interesting."

"And Willy is interesting?"

"His past, Mrs. Murkin, his checkered past. The poor devil has seen it all. He has no idea how fascinating tales of various stays behind bars can be." He stopped and looked at her with his brows raised. "You know all that, don't you?"

"Of course."

"But of course you would. I don't want to spread scandal. I don't think the others know. Needless to say, Willy swore me to secrecy."

"And you've become friends."

"We are close enough that I fear for him. The little business with my computer fills me with apprehension. That little man could be in danger, Mrs. Murkin. Who knows what animosities are formed, what plots are hatched, in minds troubled by years deprived of freedom?"

"You mean Patrick Crowe."

Mr. Walsh stopped. "Do I? Willy hasn't mentioned that name."

That put Marie in the driver's seat, and she brought Mr. Walsh up to date on the odd visit of Patrick Crowe to St. Hilary's. Mr. Walsh frowned and shook his head, and Marie had the feeling that she was confirming all his worst fears. Of course he wanted to know who Patrick Crowe was, and Marie told him what she knew.

"Mrs. Murkin, you astound me. How can you have all this at your fingertips?"

So she told him of Phil Keegan's friendship with Father Dowling and how easy it was for her to pick up the information that had impressed him.

"Gerry is Captain Keegan's nephew, his sister's child."

One would have thought that was the most interesting item she had passed on to him. They had been going back and forth on the walk, keeping out of sight of the school, but now Walsh started them back in that direction.

"I'm going to have to go home and change," he said. "I don't want to play tennis in these clothes."

"Who are you going to play tennis with?"

She half expected him to say Willy Fisk. But he sighed and lifted his brows. "Need you ask?"

And there was Agatha coming toward them, improbably clad in shorts and tank top. Her thin legs disappeared into tube socks, and the shoes she wore made slapping sounds on the walk. Timothy Walsh squeezed Marie's hand and then led Agatha off to his car.

13

Gerry asked Father Dowling if he could borrow his car, as the minibus would have been too obvious, and when he picked up Janet he went in and met her brothers. Mrs. Hospers was a different woman in her own home; no longer the brisk, efficient director of the parish center, but obviously the mother of these kids who formed her greatest interest.

"Where are you going?" Mrs. Hospers asked.

"We haven't decided," Gerry said.

"Any suggestions, Mom?"

"A movie. I don't know what's on. They have to be videos before I see them."

Carl, the older boy, showed Gerry his computer. It was one of the original IBMs that he'd picked up for a couple of dollars when one of the municipal departments upgraded their equipment. Carl had added memory and speed, a hard disk, and a modem. He had been calling in to local bulletin boards and wanted to start one of his own.

"I'd need a special phone line for that, so I suppose I'll have to wait. I tie up our phone enough as it is."

"What's a bulletin board?"

"Don't ask," Janet wailed.

But Gerry stayed for a short explanation and found himself getting really interested. Carl explained how the modem enabled him to use the phone line to contact other computers. A bulletin board provided programs and games he could download onto his computer, as well as a means of communicating with other operators. It sounded like fun.

"I wonder if Timothy Walsh has a modem in his computer, Janet."

"If you think I'm going to encourage you, you're mistaken."

"Of course, he would have to plug into a telephone to use it."

"Gerry," she said, and the warning note in her voice made her sound like her mother, "I thought we were going to check out Patrick Crowe."

"We are."

She put her hand on his arm. "I'm sorry, but Carl never shuts up about computers. It is not my favorite subject."

"What is?"

"Finding out the truth of what happened to Timothy Walsh's shoulder bag."

"You mean his computer."

She ignored that. She had a map of Fox River opened now, and she showed him where she had marked the location of Patrick Crowe's halfway house. They had figured out roughly where it was from what Gerry had overheard his uncle say to Father Dowling, but Janet hadn't known where the address was. Hence the map.

Fox River, Illinois, is directly west of O'Hare International Airport and north of Elgin, on the river from which it takes its name, a river that comes down from Wisconsin. Greater Chicago had spread south and west, engulfing what had once been basically isolated small towns. Cook County provided a common government, but the cities and towns retained local self-government. Thus their inhabitants might assert or deny that they lived in Chicago, depending on their disposition. In any case, the map showed the density of development among the towns. The halfway house in which Patrick Crowe was being prepared for full return to freedom was ten miles from the center of Fox River, in an area that seemed to have been spawned by a massive mall. Which came first, the mall or the housing developments that supplied its customers? The answer was that they had come together, the concept of the same developer. This was a part of Illinois that was in its modest way a Silicon Plain if not a Valley, home to dozens of smaller electronic manufacturers, satellites of the computer companies that were now located almost anywhere in the country from Texas to South Dakota to New Jersey, to say nothing of California. Patrick Crowe must have felt right at home.

"What do you mean?"

"Haven't I told you the story?" Gerry asked.

"I'll stop you if you have."

Apparently he hadn't. Janet listened as he drove and talked. It was still light—in fact, the setting sun was bright in the rear-view mirror—and Gerry found it easier to imagine Crowe's life as a sales representative as he drove. It was businesses like these that Crowe had represented and others like them that he had visited as clients, picking up the information that he had then passed on to the man who did the actual breaking in. The operation had been entirely in his control, except for that dependence on the break-in man. Crowe had gained knowledge of mail-order computer houses in this country as well as of places abroad that assembled the machines, and he had developed a very profitable sideline selling stolen items until he realized that suspicion had turned on him.

"That's when he got rid of the one man who could have connected him to the thefts."

"Killed him?"

"He was crushed by a lift truck that supposedly went out of control when he was helping himself to someone's warehouse. But it wasn't an accident. It's not easy to run over yourself with a forklift. And there were signs that someone else had been there with him."

"Patrick Crowe."

"That is what they managed to prove. Crowe might have stuck to his story that the whole thing was an accident, that he just happened to be in the area when he saw the warehouse lit, that he stopped by, figuring he would know who was working late, on and on. But he decided to concede he was an accomplice and was allowed to plead guilty to manslaughter and that was it. Much to my uncle's chagrin."

"And now he is walking around free."

"Renting cars."

The halfway house looked like any other suburban ranch, except that the lot wasn't a choice one, facing onto the feeder road that ran parallel to the interstate and picking up a pretty steady roar from the traffic. If the neighbors knew what the house was used for they might not have objected, since it might have stood empty if the state hadn't leased it. From what Gerry had gathered from his uncle, the practice of locating paroled prisoners in such houses in ordinary neighborhoods was not always a welcome one to the residents, particularly if recovering drug abusers were involved. But the house in which Patrick Crowe lived was populated with murderers and white-collar criminals, and so far it had escaped notice or at least complaint from the locals. It was not an ideal neighborhood in which to park and keep the house under surveillance.

The cars were all pulled into driveways and parked in front of double garages whose doors stood open, revealing the usual array of suburban paraphernalia. Father Dowling's car parked on the street would be pretty conspicuous, so Gerry went slowly past the halfway house and kept going along the suburban street.

"Maybe we should park on the feeder road."

"Do you really think a parked car would make these people nervous?"

"I'm sure they all know one another and anything unfamiliar would catch the eye."

Janet seemed to doubt this, but she said nothing. It turned out not to matter. When they were coming back toward the entrance of the development, nearing the halfway house, Janet cried out, "There he is."

Patrick Crowe had come out of the house and was waving at a Ford that had just turned in from the feeder road. The driver pulled into the driveway and Crowe hopped in. Meanwhile, Gerry had parked. They waited until the car carrying Crowe had started off, then followed it.

"The car is full," Janet said.

"I wonder who they all are."

There were four men in the car: the driver and Crowe in the front seat, two others in the back. The car took the feeder road to the first entrance to the interstate and got on it. Gerry followed.

"I wonder how far they're going."

The traffic on the interstate was thick, and the car hurtled along at seventy-five miles an hour. Father Dowling's car sounded as if it had been some time since it had hit such a speed, but Gerry didn't want to let the Ford out of sight.

The Ford passed one exit and seemed to have settled into a steady speed, as if for a long haul, but as the next exit came up, its turn signal began to flash.

"Whew," Janet said. "I was afraid we were on our way to Wisconsin."

They followed the car to a mall, where it parked outside a bowling alley. The driver opened the trunk, and the men who had been sitting in back got out bags containing bowling balls and they all started for the entrance.

"What's that legend on the back of their shirts?"

"I couldn't see," Gerry said. "You think we better go in?"

"Isn't that why we're here?"

But who would have thought it was to watch four middle-aged men bowl? The legend on their shirts was INCARNATION, and below, in smaller letters, COURTESY OF BINKSKI'S FUNERAL HOME.

"The parish team?"

"Looks like it."

"Maybe we ought to challenge them in the name of St. Hilary's."

At least Janet was a good sport about it. This was pretty obviously a wasted night so far as turning up anything suspicious about Patrick Crowe was concerned.

"Maybe he's really reformed."

"Yeah. 'I'll never kill again.' "

Three more nights that week they kept an eye on Patrick Crowe. The second night he was umpire at a softball game involving the Incarnation women's team. The third night he stayed home. Or so it seemed. They parked on the feeder road, letting the motor run so they could listen to the radio, and when ten o'clock arrived they were ready to call it a night.

"Just a couple of nights prove nothing," Janet said loyally.

"It's not scientific. We would have to have twenty-four-hour round-the-clock surveillance and over an indefinite period."

"If that's true, we are really wasting our time."

The door of the house opened, throwing a cone of light onto the grass, which widened as the door opened and fell briefly on the driveway, where one of the rental cars was parked. There had been only a silhouette in the doorframe, but when the car door was opened and the interior lights went on, the man who slipped behind the wheel was definitely Patrick Crowe. Gerry already had Father Dowling's car in gear and was ready to go.

Crowe backed out of the driveway but did not turn on the headlights until he was in the street. When he reached the feeder road, he turned in their direction and they ducked out of sight. Gerry was holding his breath and Janet must have been too, because all he heard was the thump of his own heart. Crowe's car seemed to be moving very slowly when it went past, but then they heard it pick up speed.

Gerry had to go ahead in order to turn around, but soon they were barreling after Crowe.

"Aren't you going to put on the lights, Gerry?"

"I can see him all right."

"I was thinking of cars that can't see us."

Crowe had taken a turn, and Gerry put his lights on before following. Whatever his destination, Crowe seemed content with the suburban streets, where not much speed was possible. But then he came to a county road and turned west.

"Is he going back to Fox River?"

That was his destination, all right, and once in town the route he took was familiar.

"He's going to St. Hilary's!" Janet cried.

Feeling foolish, Gerry followed Crowe to the parish plant.

At first it looked as if he was going to stop at the rectory, but he went past, around the church, and pulled over to the curb almost exactly at the spot where he had stopped Gerry mowing and asked about Willy Fisk. Gerry circled the block and pulled the car into the rectory driveway. Janet had her door open before the sound of the motor died away.

"The school," she said.

Neither one of them had to say "Willy Fisk." They walked on the grass bordering the sidewalk leading to the school, the better to muffle the sound of their footsteps. Then Gerry grasped Janet's arm and stopped her. A flashlight beam was coming along the side of the school building, illuminating the feet of the person approaching. Every twenty yards the light would go off, and there would be total darkness and silence. Then it would switch on again, and Crowe would be on the move.

He rounded the corner of the building and turned off the flashlight. The light from a streetlamp was more than enough for him now. He went past the double doors that led into the gym, which during the day was the main gathering place, and continued to the single metal door with the narrow window of meshed glass that led to the basement. The flashlight went on and they saw the glint of metal, and then the faintest sound came to them.

"Does he have a key?" Janet asked.

If he did, it wasn't the right one. Five minutes went by, the flashlight turning on and off, Crowe seeming to be trying other keys. And then he had it. The light went out, and though he opened it with the greatest of care, they heard the basement door give. Of course, they were concentrating on it. Silence enveloped them. There was no longer anyone by the basement door.

"He's inside," Gerry said.

"What are we going to do?"

"Come on."

He took her hand and, bending over, moved swiftly across the lighted corner of the playground and into the darkness at the far side of the school. There was a row of pines on that side of the school, and suddenly two of them were illuminated as the lights in Willy Fisk's basement apartment went on. They got to the window in time to see Crowe crouched just inside the door, looking around wildly. He must have entered the room intending to surprise Fisk and now realized it was empty.

For several minutes, Crowe checked out the room, a look of disgust on his face, but that seemed directed at himself. Before he left, he stood by the door, looking around once more, his hand on the light switch. Then there was darkness.

Gerry and Janet stayed where they were. A few minutes later, at the sound of a motor starting, they moved to the front of the building and saw Crowe drive away. Gerry lifted his eyes and saw the dimly illuminated room on the third floor where Willy Fisk spent the night.

14

Cy Horvath, lieutenant in the Fox River police detective bureau, and protégé of Phil Keegan, had been an athlete of almost professional ability in high school and during the two years he had spent at the University of Illinois on a scholarship. Almost professional. Every golf course, every tennis court, in every community in the land has members whose play rivals that of the course pro. Once they were within a whisker of entering the storied ranks where millions are made and, more important, reputations that survive in the halls of fame of the various sports. Almost. But it hadn't happened. At forty-one, Cy played tennis several times a week and had been Fox River amateur champion in three divisions thus far. He was a scratch golfer whose game seemed lifted from a video on how to do it right. Almost professional, but not quite. An injury had put him out of football; he had tried baseball as a walk-on, but the cartilage damage in his leg doomed his efforts to make the team as a catcher. His scholarship was withdrawn, he left school, and Phil Keegan suggested he join the force. Keegan had been his mentor ever since. Maybe that's why Cy felt half jealous of Keegan's cousin Gerry, who seemed to be playing detective himself and with a girlfriend in tow.

Cy had been assigned to keep an eye on Patrick Crowe, so

in the last several weeks he had spent a lot of time at the Fox River airport, assuring himself that Crowe had indeed been coming to work and putting in his eight hours. Crowe's attendance was so flawless, Cy began to find that suspicious, and he spelled the swing-shift squad every other night—not telling Keegan, as this was something he wanted to do—and found Crowe living by the book, chapter and verse. All other reports confirmed this.

"Well, Cy, he was a white-collar criminal," said Keegan, "until he got frightened into killing his accomplice."

"So what do you mean?"

"He's got a suburban mentality. It's no act. That's the life he was dreaming about in Joliet. Eight hours, then home for the night."

"He goes bowling, he officiates at games," Cy argued.

"Parish stuff. It's the same thing."

"You think he's reformed?"

"No."

"So what do you mean?"

"Watching a man like Patrick Crowe won't accomplish a thing. He isn't going to sneak out some night and rob a bank or stick up a liquor store. Any crime he commits will be as slick as the one that did him in before. Inside information on something he can turn to a quick profit with a minimum of complications."

Cy went on keeping Crowe under surveillance anyway. No matter what Keegan said, Cy tended to think there was only one kind of criminal, and that was the stupid kind. Every criminal seemed determined to hang himself. Cy was sitting in an unmarked car parked in the driveway of an assistant prosecutor when he saw the two kids drive past the halfway house, obviously looking it over. It was when he recognized the car as Father Dowling's that Cy put two and two together: Gerry Krause, and the girl with him was Janet Hospers.

They followed Crowe and his team to the bowling alley, the next night they went to a softball game and watched Patrick Crowe umpire. Watching the two kids waste their time made Cy feel less foolish about wasting his own. But the third night the kids showed up, something happened.

Cy let Gerry follow Crowe closely, and he held back. When Crowe headed for Fox River and then seemed to be zeroing in on St. Hilary's, Cy wondered if Crowe hadn't spotted the kids and decided to lead them on a chase. Take them right back to where they'd come from. Funny. Cy saw everything that happened at the school, knew that Crowe had broken into the basement apartment that should have been occupied by Willy Fisk, and received rather than gave a surprise.

The two kids called it a night after that, but Cy followed Crowe when he drove away. He drove aimlessly, as if he were trying to figure out what had happened, then began to move faster. He ended up at the bar of the bowling alley where his team had won for Incarnation a few nights before. Cy doubted that anyone in the bar would have mistaken Crowe for a parish bowler.

The bar was a technical violation of parole, but Crowe might have chosen it so that he could point out that this is where he bowled, and didn't he have a few beers then, so what was the big deal? Not that Cy intended to turn him in as a parole violator. Crowe's nocturnal trip to St. Hilary's school and apparent attempt to surprise Willy Fisk had opened up a new avenue.

It had been opened up when Gerry identified the man who had stopped by to ask about Willy Fisk as Patrick Crowe, except that the stakeout man on Crowe at the time claimed that Crowe had taken his usual route from the airport to the halfway house. He could be lying or simply making an assumption from past experience or telling the truth for that matter. Gerry wouldn't be the first one who had identified the wrong person. Now Cy knew that Gerry had been right. But what connection was there between Fisk and Crowe? He got on that the following day.

Joliet was the obvious link. Fisk had been sent up for burglary while Patrick Crowe was doing time, and while there was no recorded link between the two before that common stay in Joliet, prison was a great leveler, bringing together all kinds of unlikely and different feathered birds. The only trouble with the theory was that Axelson, the warden at Joliet, with whom Cy discussed the matter, was adamant that the two men had not been friendly at Joliet.

"Okay, not friends. But they would have known one another."

"You mean one man knowing who the other was and vice versa, though not talking or getting together or anything?"

"Yeah."

"Cy, that may be true of everyone here."

"I see what you mean."

"You want me to keep asking around?"

"No, Arnie, thanks. You've been a big help."

"I have?"

"Even No is an answer."

"You sound like my girlfriend."

"I'll bet I don't look like her."

Arnie Axelson would have been the first to stress the enormous discretion prisoners exhibit. Communication is possible with almost no detectable sign of it. In any case, as often as not, inmates who had been connected outside the walls won't have anything to do with one another inside, especially if they were convicted in the same case.

There was little help in such thoughts. That Fisk would have known who Patrick Crowe was and vice versa meant nothing. They may have even communicated without drawing attention to it, but that possibility was a weak reed on which to lean if he wanted to link the two. No, the link was the one Crowe had established since getting out. He had stopped by St. Hilary's and asked for Willy Fisk. And, more dangerous, in a clear violation of parole, he had been out after curfew and been guilty of breaking and entry. That was enough to send the man packing back to Joliet. Keegan listened to all of this impassively.

"One thing's clear, Cy."

"What?"

"None of this has anything to do with his threat against me."

"So I should just let it go?"

Keegan scowled. "You know that's not what I meant."

"Maybe I should have a talk with Willy?"

"No. But you might acquaint yourself with his past. Who handled his last offense? Not the prosecutor, I mean in the department."

Cy checked it out. The investigating officer of record was a man named Duffy, now retired and living in a mobile-home village on a bluff over the Fox River just west of where I-90 crossed it. His fishing hat was festooned with flies, every expression he had ever had seemed engraved on his leathery face, and he smelled of fish.

"It's good for the heart, Cy. Fish."

"I thought it was good for the brain."

"I'm too late for that."

"You remember a small-time crook named Willy Fisk?"

Duffy remembered him. Cy had read the file and was impressed by the accuracy of Duffy's memory. Fisk had been pulled over with a trunk full of stolen items in his stolen car.

"Pulled over just by accident?"

"I was the arresting officer, Cy. I never worked in Traffic."

"What put you onto him?"

"Isn't that in the file?"

Cy grinned. "The file says you got a call."

"A tip. That's right. I looked him up, found him in a stolen car with a trunk full of goodies. Easy."

"Why?"

"Why the tip that made it so easy? I wondered about that, but as I remember, Willy wasn't interested in discussing it. You know how stoic they can get once they know you've got them. I suppose it was some disgruntled lady."

"You never looked into it, though?"

"Cy, I was a cop, not a counselor for the lovelorn."

"Willy never married."

"He didn't have time. Or he was always doing time." Duffy glanced toward the mobile home, in the shade of which his wife sat reading a large shiny paperback. "Not that marriage ain't like doing time, eh, Cy?"

15

Father Dowling did not bring up the matter of how Gerry was using his car after Cy Horvath passed him the word. Cy hadn't told Phil Keegan, and he certainly wasn't suggesting that the pastor of St. Hilary's rein in his summer boarder and assistant groundskeeper.

"I suppose it's listening to Uncle Phil talking that put it in his head, Father."

"Marie Murkin thinks living here will turn him into a priest, not a policeman."

Roger Dowling liked having Gerry around. He was company in the house, and he was essential to keeping the grounds looking well. If nothing else was known about Willy Fisk, it was that he was lazy. Time had been so often for him simply duration, something to live through, looking forward to release and freedom; now that he was on his own again he might just as well have been whiling away his life in a cell in Joliet.

Cy had told him the circumstances of Fisk's arrest on the occasion that had sent him to Joliet most recently. Had the little fellow brooded about betrayal during his sentence rather than about his own folly in committing the crime that put him there? Some people do seem to have a penchant for bad luck, and Fisk was clearly one of them. Add to that the stupidity of thinking he could help himself to the goods of others with impunity and you have an unfortunate combination indeed. But if anyone was acting stupidly now it was Patrick Crowe.

Stopping by and asking for Fisk might have been dismissed as what Phil Keegan had taken it for: showing off his car and apparent prosperity to someone who had seen him in reduced circumstances. But the message he had left for Fisk with Gerry was silly or foolish, and whatever else Father Dowling had heard of Patrick Crowe it was not that he was a fool.

As far as Father Dowling understood, Crowe had devised a very ingenious and effective organization, to rob warehouses of electronic items essential for personal computers and then to market them with the sleazy marginal dealers in this country and those abroad. One of the mystifying aspects of criminal activity like that in which Patrick Crowe had engaged is that a similar amount of thought and energy directed along unforbidden lines could lead to legitimate success. Of course, capital has to be attained, a foothold; but surely someone who could overcome the obstacles in the way of successful criminal activity could surmount those to be found in the sunnier arena of the licit. Doubtless the attraction is that one could deal in what one had not made and incur expenses of laughably minimum level in operating outside the law. The continuing specter of apprehension, until the blow fell, would be a stimulus as well as a depressant.

"I was framed, Father," Willy Fisk said when Father Dowling asked the little fellow about his most recent misadventure with the law.

"By whom?"

Fisk turned his head and looked at the priest from the

corner of his eye. "I'm not sure I'd tell you that even in the confessional, Father."

"Do you know?"

"Think about it, Father. I was driving a borrowed car, I admit it, and if I'd been stopped for speeding and it just came out that the car wasn't mine, well, things happen. Sure they're going to find the stuff in the trunk once I'm pulled over, so I know from the outset I'm a dead duck. But I know too it couldn't have been any accident."

"Then you do know who phoned the police?"

"There are things that just aren't said, Father Dowling, not even years after."

"Honor among thieves?"

Fisk laughed. "Nothing so noble. Everybody hates a squealer."

"I think I know who it was, Willy."

Fisk held up both hands. "Don't guess, Father. There's no point in it."

"So you're protecting a squealer to avoid becoming one yourself?"

Fisk smiled. "That's right. I never thought of it like that, but you're right. That makes me better than him, doesn't it?"

"Him?"

"Whoever."

"Are you comfortable on the third floor, Willy?"

"Sure. It's fine. Kind of lonely, but then it isn't crowded in that basement apartment at night when everyone's gone home."

Strange little man. Back at the rectory, Father Dowling got out the mimeographed form he'd had Fisk fill out before he hired him. It had been devised by Edna Hospers for use by the part-time help she hired during the summer. Fisk had managed not to mention his brushes with the law, but then

Father Dowling already knew all about them. For previous employment, Fisk had listed D-Mart. D-Mart was a local discount house with outlets in two or three of the lesser malls. The item stuck in his memory, and that evening, when he and Gerry were talking about Fisk, he was able to answer a question Gerry put to him. They had been discussing how odd it was to know that Fisk had been paid the surprise visit he had been worried enough about to move to the nurse's room on the third floor, and he didn't even know it. Only half a dozen people did, besides Patrick Crowe, of course. As they sat talking, they knew that the school was being closely watched by relays of squad cars and by one special officer located they knew not where but in view of the school. If Patrick Crowe was stupid enough to repeat what he had done before, he would be on his way back to Joliet.

"I almost feel I should warn him, Gerry."

"Tell him not to violate his parole? He already knows that."

"Earlier, when his scheme was detected, he had a feeling the police were closing in on him. That is when the unfortunate accident to his accomplice occurred."

"Was it an accident?"

"It was officially. That's why Patrick Crowe got out of prison as soon as he did. I wonder if he senses now that his movements are being watched."

"You sound like you hope he does."

"What good, to him or anyone else, would sending him back to prison serve?"

"He's not entirely out yet, is he?"

"Maybe they bring it with them. Willy certainly has. People think monks lead a tough life, but it's hardly any tougher than the one Willy leads. He might just as well be in a cell."

"Why did you hire him?"

"He needed a job."
"Where did he work before?"
"On his application, he mentioned D-Mart."
"D-Mart!"
"It's a discount store. They carry everything."
"Oh, I know what it is."

16

Janet missed going on surveillance duty with Gerry, although it was nice to get a good night's sleep for a change. By agreement, she hadn't told her mother about Patrick Crowe's breaking in to the school. That had been aimed at Willy Fisk and nothing else, so it seemed all right not to tell her mother. Besides, the police were watching the school now, and any repetition would bring a surprise to Patrick Crowe. The fact that Willy Fisk himself did not know was the curious thing.

"I told my uncle neither of us would tell him," Gerry said.

"You promised for me?"

"If you want to put it that way."

She didn't mind, of course, not really, but she was glad she said it because Gerry became apologetic, agreeing that he should have spoken to her first.

"I wouldn't want you to do that for me."

"I don't think I would have told Willy anyway. It still burns me that you do the work he's hired to do."

"If he did it I'd be out of a job."

"It would make more sense to put him out of a job."

"Where would he go?"

"I don't know."

"How about D-Mart?"

"D-Mart?" Janet repeated.

"It's where he worked before."

"So what are you grinning like that for?"

"It was one of the places to which Patrick Crowe sold his stolen electronics."

"How do you know that?"

"Father Dowling asked to see the file on Patrick Crowe, and Uncle Phil brought it to the rectory and they let me see it. I'd never seen anything like that before, so I really studied it. My memory is pretty good, you know, but even if it weren't I think I would have remembered D-Mart."

"You think they worked together?"

"There's more."

"What?"

"The stolen goods found in the car Willy was arrested in," Gerry replied.

"What stolen goods? Where are you finding out all these things?"

"Cy Horvath told me about this. Willy was stopped driving a stolen car and they found stolen stuff in the trunk. Electronic stuff. I want to see Willy's file. I'll bet anything that what they found in the trunk was stuff Crowe had stolen."

Janet sat back, shaking her head. "Uh-uh. Patrick Crowe was already in jail when Willy was arrested."

"You're sure of that?"

"As sure as I am of anything Willy tells me. That came out right after Patrick Crowe stopped you on the mower and sent that message to Willy. He said Crowe had already been in prison when Willy got there."

"Well, I'll get to see Willy's file anyway. My uncle promised to bring it to the house."

"Does he know we were watching Crowe?"

"He has to. But he pretends not to. He can hardly approve, but I think he likes the fact that we did."

"I suppose he thinks it runs in the family."

"Maybe it does."

Gerry went off to the maintenance shed, and a minute later she heard the mower start up. Things were pretty noisy until he went out of sight around the building. Mr. Walsh came toward her, his fingers stuck in his ears, a pained expression on his face.

"He's off murdering grass again, I see." He took his fingers out of his ears. "I mean, I hear." He adjusted his shoulder bag.

"My brother is a hacker, Mr. Walsh," Janet told him.

The fine white brows rose above his glasses. "A hacker?"

"A computer buff. He has an old one he rebuilt and upgraded until it does everything but contact the moon. I suppose you know what a modem is."

"He has one, does he?"

"I wish he didn't. He ties up the phone."

"Ah well," said Mr. Walsh. "And what does your mother have planned for us today?"

Janet felt a little put down. Mr. Walsh showed no interest at all in Carl's computer or modem, and that surprised her, given the fuss he had made over his machine when it was missing. But she found it hard to worry about that, given the exciting possibility that Gerry had turned up.

More than a possibility, as they learned. Gerry's hunch turned out to be the flat truth of the matter. He called to tell her what he had discovered on Willy Fisk's police record. There was an itemized list of the articles discovered in the stolen car Fisk had been driving when arrested. All were computer parts, and all had come from the warehouse of one of the companies whose inventory Crowe had known about because of his day-time business dealings with the firm.

"Then they must have been partners, Gerry."

"It looks like it."

"So why is Crowe breaking into Willy's apartment?"

"Are you due to use the minibus tomorrow?"

"I have to drive anyone who's interested to the mall."

"They get back on their own, don't they?"

"No. I give them two hours or two and a half and then pick them up again."

"That ought to be enough time."

"For what?"

"I'll tell you tomorrow."

"Gerry! I hate secrets."

"We're going to talk to the man who arrested Willy."

"Why don't we just talk to Willy?"

"I want to know more than I do now before we talk to him."

Gerry was already on the mower when Janet and her mother arrived at the parish center the next morning.

"Couldn't you sleep?" she asked him, after he had finished half the lawn and was taking a break.

"I want to be through here when we leave. When is the excursion to the mall?"

"We leave at noon."

"I'll be ready."

And he was, but so were nine prospective shoppers—a full load for the minibus, and Gerry had to stand in front next to her. The excited chirping voices of the passengers continued through the drive. Pointing out landmarks, recalling how a neighborhood or building looked twenty-five years ago or more was a favorite practice.

"I remember when this whole area was farmland," someone said when they turned in to the mall.

"Before you know it there won't be any farms left."

"And we'll be importing food from Japan."

That started an argument that was still going on after Janet had made clear when she would return and they were off.

"Where to?" she asked Gerry.

"We're a lot closer to it now than we were at St. Hilary's."

It was a trailer park, and the man who had agreed to talk with them was a retired detective named Duffy. He would have spent the whole time telling Gerry about what a grand fellow his uncle was if Gerry hadn't insisted on turning the conversation to the arrest of Willy Fisk.

"Someone blew the whistle on him, sure."

"Why would they do that?"

"I've got a guess," Duffy said.

"What is it?"

"First I ought to tell you the official theory. Willy had a girlfriend in those days, a woman named Ruth. Willy called her 'Ruthless,' and he might have been right. When they weren't making up, they were fighting, and the theory was that she had turned Willy in. Revenge. A scorned woman. That sort of thing. Willy wouldn't say yes or no, but he liked the idea so much everyone assumed that's what happened."

"What's your own guess?" Gerry asked.

Duffy's guess turned on Fisk's righteous refusal to speculate on who it was that had called the police and set up the arrest that landed Willy in Joliet. "He kept saying he wouldn't be a squealer. My guess is that that's just what he was and that's why they squealed on him."

"Did the police receive a tip on Patrick Crowe?"

"Crowe? I thought we were talking about Willy Fisk."

"Did you ever have any reason to link him with Patrick Crowe?"

"Crowe's the manufacturer's rep who ripped off the companies he dealt with." Duffy might have been reminding himself. "I didn't work on that. Your uncle handled that. He would have nailed Crowe for murder one if the prosecutor hadn't been so eager for a conviction and let Crowe plea bargain."

"This is a pleasant place," Janet said after a while, looking over the grassy expanse to the river.

"We like it. I get homesick, I can just drift downstream and be in Fox River the city."

Their business was over, but since they still had time they went down to the river with Duffy to admire the aluminum boat in which he did his fishing.

"Your wife go with you?"

"And miss her programs? No way. It's the secret of a happy marriage."

"Fishing?"

"Separate interests. I watch television during the daytime I get a headache. My wife claims that sitting in a boat makes her ill. We're perfectly matched."

Janet noticed that Gerry didn't tell Duffy about his own hunches, although he had asked the leading question about a link between Fisk and Crowe. But Duffy had not risen to the bait. Of course there was still a missing piece to the puzzle.

"When will you ask your uncle if someone informed on Patrick Crowe?" she asked him as they were leaving.

"As soon as I can. He came by the rectory last night and we watched the Sox with Father Dowling. There was talk of going to the Cubs tonight but he wasn't sure."

Gerry seemed as sure as she was of the answer to the question he would put to Captain Keegan. Patrick Crowe had been in prison when the informant's call led to the arrest of Willy Fisk. If Fisk had informed on his old partner, his own arrest in turn would have been a matter of Crowe getting even.

"Only he doesn't seem to think they're even yet," Gerry said.

17

"I feel as if I'm working in the state prison," Marie Murkin said, commenting on all the goings-on around the parish of late.

She had grumbled when the pastor hired Willy Fisk, but she'd held her tongue outside the rectory lest Edna Hospers misunderstood and think some reference were being made to her absent husband. Still and all, Marie wondered if Father Dowling would have been that receptive to the suggestion that Willy Fisk find his way back to responsible citizenship via employment at St. Hilary's. Employment! Any work done around the place was done by Gerry Krause, and Father Dowling knew that as well as she did.

"Gerry likes the job, Marie," Phil Keegan protested. "He isn't complaining, why should you?"

"I was making an observation, not complaining, Captain Keegan."

Of course he would speak for his nephew with the boy right there, ignoring them both as he looked over the papers his uncle had brought him. All this curiosity about police work added to Marie's sense that the whole tone of the parish was being altered. Sometimes she wished Father Dowling had never had the idea of turning the school into a parish center. Oh, it had been sad seeing the place stand empty, with grass growing in the cracks of the playground and the empty windows staring bleakly at nothing, with never a living face looking out of them. It was selfish to wish there was nothing but the noon Mass and whatever chance visitor there might be. Father Dowling could sit in his study and smoke his pipe and read his books more than he did now, and she could concentrate on cooking and not worry about what was going on over at the school, particularly with the likes of Willy Fisk living over there in the basement apartment.

Phil Keegan was taking Gerry off to the Cubs game and the pastor was going into Chicago to take part in the closing of a Forty Hours. *Leaving me with the jailbirds,* Marie thought, but of course she did not say it aloud.

She locked up the rectory tightly and climbed the backstairs to her own quarters and would have felt safe but for the thought that only a short distance away, in the school, was Willy Fisk, probably getting drunk and watching television. As far as Marie could make out, no one had told him of the man breaking into the basement apartment. That didn't bother her, and anyway it seemed for the best, since nothing further had happened and the school continued to be under close surveillance.

She said her prayers and read her novel and then turned off the light, but before sleep came she thought that now would be a good time to clean up that basement apartment. Willy didn't spend much time in it during the day, and at night he would be making a mess of the nurse's office on the third floor. As is the way with such thoughts, once it came she could not rid herself of it, and she lay sleepless thinking how satisfying it would be to make that apartment as spick-and-span as it had been when Fisk moved into it. Cleaning it had the added advantage of making it clear that she considered the school itself part of her responsibility. Let Edna run the programs, that was all well and good; but the school, like the church, came under the ultimate jurisdiction of Marie Murkin.

This comforting thought brought on sleep. In the morning, what with getting Gerry's breakfast and then trying to persuade Father Dowling to take something more than toast and coffee, Marie had actually started the laundry before she remembered the basement apartment in the school. She glanced out the window, and it was clear that the day's programs were well under way. Edna was a punctual soul, and that is a great virtue in someone directing a program. Starting and ending on time, no matter what the function, gave a note of authority.

Marie did two loads of laundry and had the second in the dryer when she set out for the school, moving briskly along the walk that joined the rectory and parish center. As she walked, she imagined those poor retired souls seeing her and envying her her purposeful day. She assumed a serious expression to convey the number and extent of her duties and responsibilities. As she went through the gym, she slowed her pace, willing to be stopped and asked whatever might be troubling the person in question. Marie considered herself to be on the pastoral staff, and she was ever ready to give such counseling as might be required.

But none was required this morning. She left the auditorium and entered the corridor and a moment later stood at the door of the basement apartment. She knocked briskly, frowning at the panel. No answer came. Marie looked sternly up and down the hallway, grasped the door handle, and turned. It was unlocked. She left the door standing open and went in.

"Mr. Fisk?" she called. "Mr. Fisk?"

Fisk had not been in evidence outside, but Marie was not sure she should credit stories that he lay abed until ten and then wandered down hoping to make a breakfast of the doughnuts and rolls brought with them by the old folks. He was certainly not in this apartment. The thought of cleaning the place was less attractive than it had been the night before. Did it really matter that she assert her authority in the school? More to the point, would it matter if she got this place in order? Fisk would turn it into a hovel before nightfall. The neatness that had been forced upon him in prison had apparently called forth this slovenly reaction, and Marie doubted that a good scrubbing and cleaning could change Fisk, no matter what effect it had on this apartment.

The envelope was propped on the coffee table. Printed on it, apparently in crayon, was the ragged legend READ ME. Marie stooped to take it, then stopped herself. Vague memories of Alice in Wonderland suggested that she was taking part in a joke being played on herself. She looked around sharply, as if to surprise Fisk and his accomplices, ready to see her take the bait. But she was alone. The corners of her mouth were downturned, and she was frowning with disapproval when she opened the envelope. Inside was another printed crayon message: CHECK TRUNK OF CAR. That was all.

Marie stood staring at the piece of paper she held in her hands. She turned it over, she read the four words again. She had no idea what they might mean, nor whether she should take the message seriously. There was certainly no reason to think that she was the intended reader of the message. There came a tap on the door, and Marie wheeled as if she had been discovered doing something questionable. The door was unlocked so whoever had knocked would soon do as she had done—try the door to see if it was locked. Marie went to the door and pulled it open. A startled Mrs. Meade jumped up and brought her hand to her throat.

"God have mercy, you scared me!" She tried to laugh but could not.

"I am cleaning the apartment."

"I'm looking for Agatha."

"Agatha!"

"Yes, I was told I would find her here."

"By whom?"

"He didn't say. It was a phone call."

So Mrs. Meade must have been intended to find the letter. Marie went back to the coffee table and picked up the message where she had dropped it. A moment later she was sailing down the hall toward Edna Hospers's office. Whatever Willy Fisk was up to she was going to put a stop to it.

Edna was not in her office. From outside came the roar of the tractor. In a corner of the playground, Janet was washing the minibus.

"Mrs. Murkin, what is it?"

Mrs. Meade had come with her. Marie Murkin did not like being observed as confused as she now was.

"I'll take care of it, Mrs. Meade."

"But where is Agatha?"

Anyone who had attempted to waylay Marie Murkin this time as she went through the auditorium would have been rudely rebuffed. Whatever was going on, she intended to let Father Dowling figure it out. She had enough to do taking care of the rectory without bothering her head about missing maintenance men, odd notes, and phone calls to Mrs. Meade. She diverted herself to Janet and thrust the note at her.

"What do you make of this?"

Janet dried her hands on her jeans and took the paper. A little smile formed as she read it. "I give up. What is it?"

"I found it in Willy Fisk's room."

Janet thought about that. If the girl laughed or made fun, Marie would never forgive her.

"I wonder if that's the car it means. It's Mr. Walsh's."

Janet started for the car, which was parked at the opposite end of the playground, what had become Mr. Walsh's spot since he'd started driving to the center. The roar of the tractor crescendoed on a gust of wind but then subsided. They stood looking at the trunk of the car. The keys were in the lock. Janet bent forward, listening, then she opened the trunk. Marie was beside her as sun flooded into the cavity. Lying in the trunk, blindfolded, gagged, her arms and legs bound, was Agatha.

18

When Marie burst into his study, babbling like a madwoman, Father Dowling calmed her down as best he could. She was tugging him to the window and pointing toward the school. There was a little crowd forming around the back of a car with an open trunk. The mower stood abandoned in the middle of the lawn and Gerry was helping Janet lift something from the trunk. What Marie was trying to say began to make sense. Before he left the study, Father Dowling made a hurried phone call, leaving a message for Captain Keegan.

"You should call an ambulance," Marie cried.

He handed her the phone. "You do that."-

And then he was out of the house and running across the lawn. The passenger door of the car had been swung open and Janet was urging Agatha to sit down. The handkerchief that had been bound across her mouth hung loosely at her throat, and her heavily sprayed hair was arranged wildly. She rolled her eyes at the waiting passenger seat and let out a scream, falling back into Janet's arms. They carried her into some shade and Janet began to pat Agatha's forehead with a damp cloth, then stopped.

"I was washing the van with this," she said to no one in particular.

"Marie has called an ambulance," said Father Dowling.

The next forty-five minutes were the most exciting the parish center had provided its clientele all summer. Paramedics performed to the *ohs* and *ahs* of the admiring spectators. Agatha, forced into inaction but apparently no worse for wear, turned her head toward the crowd. When she grasped that it was her they were all staring at it, she emitted a theatrical sigh and brought the back of her wrist to her forehead.

"Don't move, lady," she was advised.

Agatha was still there when Cy Horvath arrived. Marie, very much a part of the inner ring, handed Cy the letter she had found in the basement apartment. With a grim look on her face, she watched him read it. She waited for his reaction. Cy Horvath's face was equipped with a single unrevealing expression used on all occasions.

"You will find him on the third floor," she said, lifting her shoulders.

"Who?"

"Willy Fisk."

Cy looked at Father Dowling, then at Marie.

"I found that note on the coffee table of the basement apartment when I went in to clean it. 'Check trunk of car.' Well, we checked and there was Agatha. Some joke."

"Joke?"

"Father Dowling will explain." Marie gave up. She did not intend to spend the rest of her morning standing here explaining matters to a detective lieutenant of the Fox River police. Cy watched the housekeeper as she marched off toward the rectory.

"She mad at me?"

Father Dowling did not blame Marie for being upset. What had happened was confusing enough, even if one had not wandered into the middle of it as Marie had. The paramedics wanted to take Agatha to the hospital, just to be sure she was as unharmed by her experience as she seemed, but first she insisted on talking to Father Dowling.

"This is Lieutenant Horvath," Father Dowling said when Agatha looked uneasily at Cy.

"A policeman?"

"Yes, ma'am."

"Oh good. I want you to hear this too. I have never been so frightened in my life."

That morning when she looked out her window she found to her surprise that Timothy Walsh's car was already parked at her curb.

"He had formed the habit of picking me up and bringing me here," Agatha said, lowering her eyes for a moment. "This morning he was early. Or my clock was late. Well, I hurried and went outside and found the car empty. But the door had been opened. Rather than just stand there, I got in. Oh, Father." She pressed her hand to her mouth and she was no longer acting. "It was horrible! First I was blinded, then that kerchief was tied over my mouth. It all happened so fast!"

Bound, gagged, blindfolded, Agatha heard someone get into the car. The motor started, and off they went.

"After a time, the car came to a stop. The driver got out. I heard the trunk open. Father, I was terrified. I didn't know what was happening. Whatever was going on in back, soon the door beside me opened. I was led around the car and the next thing I was tumbled in and the door closed over me." Agatha's eyes rounded with horror. She might have been describing her own entombment.

Cy read back to her what he had gotten, and this gave Agatha the opportunity to embellish the story.

"Wouldn't you know I'd be wearing a dress like this?" It

was filmy and yellow, very much a party dress, not the usual attire for those who came to the center. But then not all the ladies were picked up of a morning by Timothy Walsh.

It was of Timothy Walsh that Cy was thinking, of course.

"Want to come along, Father?"

He looked at his watch. The time of his noon Mass was drawing near and he couldn't take the chance of being away and unable to return.

"Can I come, Lieutenant?" Gerry asked, pressing forward.

"Good idea," Father Dowling said. "How about it, Cy?"

"Let's go."

Edna Hospers herded her wards back to the school, their chirping voices indicating that they would have more than enough to talk about for weeks. Nothing this exciting had ever happened during the lifetime of the parish center, but Father Dowling had the sense that it was but the latest in a series.

The series began, perhaps, when he had overcome whatever misgivings he had, perhaps prompted to do so by Marie Murkin's obvious disapproval, and hired Willy Fisk to look after the grounds and buildings. This made it sound a good deal more demanding than it was. What Father Dowling had in mind was sweeping the hallways of the school and trimming the grass. That second duty had to be excluded when it was clear that nothing would induce Fisk to start up, let alone mount and drive, the tractor mower. If he pushed a broom up and down the school corridors once or twice a week, that was the extent of his labor.

But with Fisk had come, besides the need to hire Gerry to do the lawns and shrubs, the mysterious visit from Patrick Crowe and then the night-time break-in when Crowe had apparently intended to do some mischief to the little man. Why? More pressing still was the message found in the basement apartment, which had led to the discovery of the bound and gagged Agatha in the trunk of Timothy Walsh's car and, Walsh being nowhere in sight, to the departure of Cy Horvath and Gerry to his home. That Walsh was not there was made known to Roger Dowling by a phone call from Phil Keegan, which had been rerouted from the house to Edna's office.

"It could be a kidnapping, Roger."

"What on earth for?"

"You tell me. The way Cy tells it, Willy Fisk seems mixed up in this."

"I was just going to talk to him."

"I intend to do the same thing."

"You might join me for lunch, Phil."

"I might come to the noon Mass too."

In any case, Father Dowling meant to have a talk with Willy Fisk before he headed for the church. It was not yet eleven-thirty. He had seen Fisk in the doorway of the school, watching the activity at Walsh's automobile but not joining the curious crowd. The pastor had checked the basement apartment, found it empty, and thought it might be a good idea to lock it, given the discovery of the message there by Marie Murkin. He had stopped by the office and received the call from Keegan.

"Have you seen Willy since things settled down, Edna?"

"He's probably hiding out in the basement apartment."

"Where else might he be?"

Her eyes lifted to the ceiling. "The third floor?"

Going up the stairs, Father Dowling could not help thinking of the generations of children who had hurried up and down these staircases, busy about growing up and going on, passing from grade to grade, different rooms marking their passage through the school, until they ended in one of the portraits of graduating classes that adorned the hallways of the school. Some of the old people who came to take part in Edna's programs had been students here in the long ago.

The location of the nurse's office on the third floor was a mystery. Perhaps it had been thought that any student able to make the climb was well enough to stay in school. Father Dowling rapped on the door with one hand and gripped the handle in the other.

"It's open."

Fisk sat in a straight-backed chair, staring out a window. He looked briefly at the priest, then turned back to the window.

"What's going on, Willy?"

"You tell me, Father."

"A note was found in the basement apartment, written in crayon."

"Mrs. Meade told me all about it."

"Timothy Walsh is missing. Phil Keegan even talked kidnapping."

"It's a good thing I'm here where you can account for me, isn't it?"

Father Dowling rolled a chair from behind the desk and sat down beside Fisk.

"I wonder if this has anything to do with Patrick Crowe, Willy."

"Crowe!"

"The other night he was here, Willy. He must have thought you were in the apartment downstairs. He let himself into the school and burst into the apartment."

Fisk listened to this with narrowed eyes. "No kidding?"

"No kidding. What if you had been there?"

"I don't know."

"Don't you?"

"I really don't."

"Then indulge me while I tell you a story."

Father Dowling laid it out for Willy as he was sure Phil Keegan would do. They now knew that Willy had been involved in the scheme that had sent Patrick Crowe to prison. The connection was D-Mart. Someone had tipped off the police on Crowe and in his nervousness his break-in man had been killed, crushed by a forklift in a warehouse where he was presumably making an unauthorized pickup. Circumstantial evidence put Crowe in that warehouse, though it might have been all but impossible to prove that. Crowe saved the state the trouble by pleading guilty to involuntary manslaughter, the bargain being that all charges of fraud and theft would be dropped. Not that Patrick Crowe was ever again likely to find work in his former profession.

"Let us say that you were the one who told the police about Patrick Crowe."

"Why would I?"

"Hear me out, Willy. I'm trying to tell you what the police are thinking. Crowe's revenge is to return the favor. The police get a call and conveniently find you in a stolen car with a trunk full of stolen items."

"Closing the account?"

"Apparently not. Why not? What does Crowe have against you, Willy?"

"I'll be damned if I know."

"Well, Willy, then I truly hope you don't know."

It was difficult to put all these things out of his mind and say his noontime Mass with devotion.

19

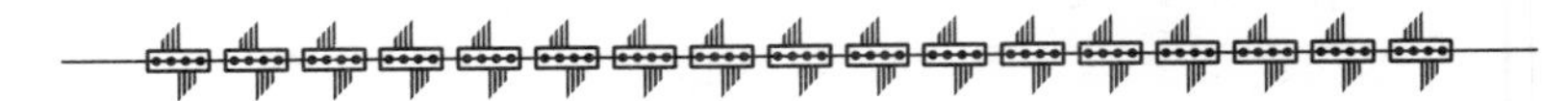

The building superintendent let them into Timothy Walsh's apartment and in a matter of minutes they determined that the place was empty. One of the bedrooms had been turned into a sort of office, and there they found a very sophisticated computer. The furniture in the room had been selected for maximum efficiency, and the place looked like an ideal workspace lifted from a computer magazine; Gerry couldn't help wonder what Carl Hospers would do with a setup like this one. The computer was on and Cy wondered about that, but Gerry passed on what Carl had told him. Many users never turn off their computer, figuring the wear on the system of heating up and cooling off frequently is potentially a far greater expense than the meager current used to keep it on.

Gerry stayed there when Cy went into the kitchen, and when he heard Cy using the phone to call in, he did a directory search. A double column of files appeared on the amber screen. Gerry's eye scanned down the first column and an item leapt out at him. At the sound of Cy's return, he hit ESCAPE and the directory faded, but he was unlikely to forget what he had seen: A file named D-MART.CRO.

It was a moment of truth. Cy had been good enough to let him come along while they checked out Walsh's apartment. By all rights he should tell him what he had just found. As far as Gerry was concerned, that file was the answer to the question why Walsh was missing. But he said nothing. He hadn't thought of the thing Cy brought up while they waited for the lab team to come and sweep the apartment.

"Your uncle thinks kidnapping."

Gerry nodded.

"Well, let's hope the guy is still alive." Cy leaned back in his chair, picked up a remote control, and turned on the TV. It had a large screen, thirty-five inches, beautiful color.

"So this is what retirement is like. Nice."

"Why would anyone kill him?" Gerry thought of the dapper little man with the snow-white hair and groomed mustache, the shoulder bag containing a compact computer ever at his side. He seemed the picture of harmlessness, but Gerry saw now, perhaps better than Cy, that that harmless little man might pose a threat.

Cy was talking of the man done in by the forklift whose death had put Crowe in Joliet for a number of years. "Of course he murdered the guy."

Gerry should have mentioned the file on the computer now, since it would save a lot of time in linking Walsh to Crowe and Fisk. Surely the lab people would check out the computer and see its significance. Gerry got to his feet, went into Walsh's office, and pulled up a directory of the hard drive. Cy came in and stood behind him.

"Better not fool around, Gerry."

"See that?" Gerry had highlighted D-MART.CRO. He called it up and waited for the screen to fill with the accounting Timothy Walsh had done for Patrick Crowe. But the screen remained blank. Puzzled, he went back to the directory. And then he noticed something he had not seen before. Beside each file was the number of bytes it took on the hard drive. Next to D-MART.CRO was 0. The file had been erased. He turned and looked up at Cy.

"It's gone. They must have wiped it out when they took him."

"What's gone?"

"A file. Some records. He worked for D-Mart, and the extension of the file name indicates this file involved Patrick Crowe."

He was saved from further explanation by the arrival of the team from the lab, a redhead named Wendy and a middle-aged man with DR. JIM on his name tag. Cy asked Gerry to tell them about the missing file. Wendy came into the office with him.

"Uh-uh-uh," she said as he was about to put his hands on the keyboard.

"I've already touched it."

"Tell me what to hit. I'll use my nails."

When she brought up the directory, Gerry pointed to the file name. "That's been erased."

"Okay."

Wendy was no more excited about it than Cy Horvath had been.

The more he thought about it, the more certain Gerry was that the missing file was the explanation of whatever had happened to Timothy Walsh.

"What did happen to him?" Janet asked later.

"Horvath wondered if he's still alive."

A pained expression came over Janet's face. "Oh no."

When he told her about the erased file on Walsh's desktop computer in his home office, she suggested they give Carl a call.

"Janet, it's been erased."

"But there are ways of retrieving files even then; Carl knows all about it."

Mrs. Hospers let them use her phone, and while Janet got Carl on the line, Gerry told Mrs. Hospers that it looked as if Timothy Walsh had been kidnapped and that his life was feared for.

"My God. Who would do such a thing?"

"I think it was Willy Fisk and Patrick Crowe."

"Gerry, here's Carl."

Gerry took the phone and explained that a file that still appeared on the directory of Walsh's hard drive had no bytes corresponding to it, could not be retrieved, and seemed to have been erased.

"You could probably get it back with Norton Utilities," Carl said. "It would be a little scrambled but maybe ninety percent okay."

"Do you have the program?"

"Norton Utilities? Sure. Want to borrow it?"

"I'd have to get permission to get back into the apartment, and then I probably wouldn't know how to do it."

"I'll come along."

Gerry and Janet picked up Carl in the minibus and headed for Walsh's apartment. The four-wheel-drive vehicle from the police lab was still in the driveway, and when they went upstairs Wendy answered the door. She looked past Gerry at Janet and Carl.

"Hey, what's this?"

"Carl here thinks he can retrieve that erased program."

Wendy shook her head. "Boy, you're pretty obsessed with that, aren't you?"

Dr. Jim appeared, looking quizzical. One side of his mouth went up and the other went down when Wendy explained.

"Tell you what. I'll deputize you, kid. See if you can retrieve it."

"The office has been dusted for prints, so don't worry," Wendy said. Gerry had wondered if she was going to offer the use of her long nails again, lest any prints on the keys be smeared. "While we're at it, I want a set of your prints so I can see if you left any here."

Gerry was rolling the balls of his fingertips over the ink-pad Wendy opened when Carl sat down at the computer. He inserted a disk into the A drive and loaded up the retrieval program, then replaced the program disk with another, and went to work, Janet looking over his shoulder.

"This is the way I look after I read the morning paper," Gerry said, displaying his ink-smeared fingers to Wendy.

"It washes right off."

"Can I use the bathroom?"

"We're all but finished. So hurry it up."

In twenty minutes, Carl was able to show Dr. Jim the spreadsheet entries that had once been called D-MART.CRO.

"I'll store it under that same name, okay?"

"Do that. Kid, you're a marvel. What grade you in?"

"Eighth. Going into."

Dr. Jim and Wendy exchanged a look.

"Any chance on taking a look at that?" Gerry asked.

"Not on my watch," Dr. Jim said. "We're out of here and so are you."

Gerry looked longingly at the screen where the retrieved spreadsheet invited perusal. He didn't know what he was looking for, but he was sure there was a clue in those figures that would explain the disappearance of Timothy Walsh.

"We'll have one of our computer nuts check it out," Wendy said.

In the minibus, Gerry said, "Maybe Lieutenant Horvath will go back there with us."

"Don't sweat it," Carl said. "I made a copy on a floppy. I'll go home and work on it and let you know if I find anything. What am I looking for?"

"I don't know."

"Right."

20

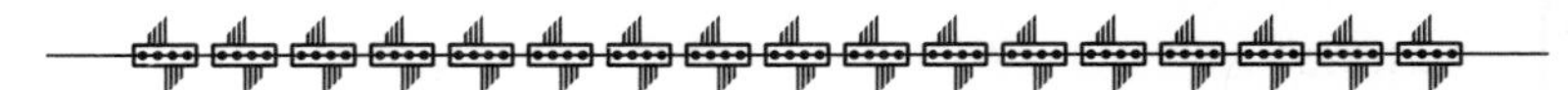

"We still got the stakeout on the school, don't we?" Phil Keegan asked. "Did Willy Fisk leave the school last night?"

Agnes Lamb, a black detective, shook her head. "He went up to the third floor at nine-thirty, his light went out at eleven, and he didn't leave the building."

"And Roger Dowling and Edna Hospers both say he was still in bed when Marie Murkin found the note. Okay, that takes care of Willy. How about Crowe?"

"He was umpire at a parish little league," Agnes replied.

"Who reported that?"

"Pianone."

"Peanuts! Was he alone?"

"He knew the score of the game, Captain. He was there. He loves baseball."

"But was Patrick Crowe there?"

"He was the umpire!"

"I guess that can be checked."

"I checked it."

Keegan looked at Agnes. Those who didn't know the captain might have interpreted his look as one of disapproval. Agnes knew better. It was the anticipation of that look that had led her to check out Peanuts's report on the whereabouts of Patrick Crowe the night before.

"Okay. So what is it that neither of those two can help us explain? Agatha looks out her window this morning and sees Timothy Walsh's car parked at the curb. He's early but otherwise she's not surprised. He has been picking her up and driving her to the parish center. When she gets out to the car, the passenger door is standing open and Walsh is not behind the wheel. This surprises her, but she gets into the passenger seat. Before she knows what's happening, she's blindfolded, gagged, and bound and taken around and put into the trunk."

"After a delay," Cy said.

Keegan thought about it. "That important?"

"Agatha heard something going on while she sat there scared out of her wits. She had heard the trunk open. Maybe they already had Walsh in the trunk and they took him out."

"I don't like it."

"Well, anyway, there was a delay."

"How many people did Agatha think were involved?"

"From one to three."

Officer Lamb tucked in her chin.

"She was very frightened. We can't rely on her for details."

"Like the delay before she was stuffed in the trunk," Keegan said. "Any sign that anyone other than Agatha was in that trunk?

Cy said, "Yes."

"Walsh?"

"Yes."

"You were just guessing before, huh?"

"Has there been a demand for ransom?" Agnes asked.

"No. Apparently they just wanted him."

"They?"

"From one to three people."

"Excluding Willy Fisk and Patrick Crowe."

"They could have paid to have it done."

"Then something should turn up."

"Yeah. Probably Walsh's body."

They went over it all several times. There was no indication that either Fisk or Crowe had contacted anyone who might have kidnapped Timothy Walsh. There was no indication that they had been in contact. Up to this point they had been proceeding on the assumption that Crowe posed a threat to Fisk.

Late in the afternoon, Crowe and Fisk were asked to come in and aid the police in the solution of a puzzling event. Patrick Crowe wanted assurance that he was not being arrested and that he was not suspected of anything. He was told to bring a lawyer if he was worried, but they would very much appreciate any help he could give them. Fisk came without any fuss. Neither knew the other had come in, and they were interviewed separately. The results did not bring joy to Keegan's heart.

"Willy said he has been getting odd phone calls from Patrick Crowe."

"Patrick Crowe said that he had been getting strange phone calls from Willy Fisk."

Crowe seemed to think that Fisk was trying to stir up trouble and he couldn't figure it out. Neither of them could afford to draw attention to themselves, and getting together spelled trouble even if there was a reason to do so. Crowe said that as far as he was concerned the past was the past and he wanted nothing to do with it.

"He volunteered the information that he had made a late-night visit to Willy to find out what the guy wanted."

Of course they knew that he had not found Fisk at home.

When the meeting adjourned, Phil Keegan had the feeling that he had just attended a wake for Timothy Walsh. When he left his office, he called the St. Hilary's rectory on his cellular phone.

"Marie, is Roger there?"

"Father Dowling?"

"This is Phil Keegan."

"Captain Keegan! How can I help you?"

Keegan gritted his teeth, wondering what he had done to bring on this high-horse attitude on the part of Marie Murkin.

"I'd like to make arrangements for a funeral."

That got her. "Are you serious?"

"Is this Mrs. Murkin? Please put me through to Father Dowling."

"Good evening, Phil. I'm on the line," the priest interrupted. "The two of you should have your own program."

"Okay if I come over?"

"Where are you?"

"Two blocks away."

Marie brought him a beer and skipped the usual comment when he got out a cigar. Minutes after settling in at the St. Hilary's rectory, his old friend Father Dowling puffing away at his pipe, Phil Keegan went through it all again. The meeting in his office had been dissatisfying, not because he had failed to mention the things they knew, or thought they knew, about recent goings-on involving Willy Fisk and Patrick Crowe, but because he was certain they were overlooking something that would seem obvious as soon as he recognized it. A talk like this with Roger Dowling was as good a way as he knew to scare the elusive fact into the open.

"How much did Patrick Crowe make from his scheme to steal computer parts from clients whose inventories he knew?"

"Cy checked that out with the prosecutor's witness who made an estimate of how much was involved. The companies took the opportunity to assign a lot of their bad debts to the thievery Crowe had been carrying on, so the numbers were spongy at best."

"How much?"

"You also have to take into account that stolen items don't bring market prices, at least not in this country. If you rent a little shed in Waco and start assembling computers, putting your name on the result, and sell them direct mail, running ads in the computer magazines, you have to cut corners to compete with the big guys. Someone like Patrick Crowe showing up with an offer of chips or transistors is the answer to a prayer. But you won't pay him what the stuff would cost you legitimately. Outside the country, who knows?"

"How much?"

"Several million."

"Where is it?"

"Roger, don't get me started. I was against letting Crowe plea bargain in the first place. Not only does he get away with murder, they accept his denial that he made anything like millions. What he had, he says, is people owing him money. Of course he kept no books."

"You mean there could be a large amount of money hidden away somewhere?"

"The watch on Crowe is not just to see that he goes to bed on time. The companies from which he stole have hired a man as well. They will have first claim to any recovered money."

"There are no records of these transactions?"

"It was a purely cash business."

Phil Keegan was at a disadvantage talking about the financial aspects of Crowe's scheme. He had lived all his life on a modest salary, and he would end his days, if he could bear to retire, on a small pension. Money in the large amounts associated with big business and professional athletics made no sense to him. But then, ever since his wife died, he had just been living from day to day, keeping busy, fighting the loneliness.

"Poor Timothy Walsh. God knows what happened to him."

"Expect the worst, Roger."

"The most curious thing to me about the whole sequence," Father Dowling said, "is the phone calls."

"Phone calls?"

The priest nodded in a cloud of tobacco smoke. "The most recent one was that received by Mrs. Meade, telling her to take a look in the basement apartment. Obviously, she was meant to find the note that Marie Murkin found."

"Someone would have found it."

"Perhaps only after poor Agatha had succumbed to terror, bad air, perhaps injuries. The caller wanted to prevent that. Convenient. It reminds me of all the other phone calls that have been received at crucial moments and caused events to go as they have gone."

Father Dowling reeled them off, and of course he was right. Cited one after another, they could look like beads on the same thread. The call that put them onto Crowe, the call that led to the arrest of Fisk.

"And now they both claim the other is calling."

"And each denies that he is doing it."

There was the sound of the door opening and a moment later being closed again before Gerry's footsteps approached them down the hallway.

"That you, Gerry?"

"Yes, Mrs. Murkin."

"Did you lock the door?"

"Yes, Mrs. Murkin."

By this time Gerry stood in the doorway of the study, his eyes bright, unable to suppress a smile. He was carrying an armload of paper.

"What is it, Gerry?"

"Something important."

21

Janet made popcorn and the three of them had settled down at Carl's computer as he brought up the file he had un-erased from the hard disk of Timothy Walsh's home computer.

"I copied another file too, so we'd have something to compare the recovered one with. There'll be garbage in it now. No recovery program is perfect."

"I think it's amazing you can find something that was erased."

"People accidentally erase things all the time, or they turn off their machines without storing and lose everything. If they do that—don't store at all—then what they were doing is lost forever. There's nowhere to look for it. But if it was once stored, even if it was erased, programs have been written to recover them. But, as I say, they're not perfect."

Janet looked at Carl as if she thought he was perfect, and Gerry felt a little twinge. Jealous? Don't be ridiculous. Besides, Carl was her brother.

"Look, why don't I print out the okay file I copied and then bring up the recovered one."

The printout made no immediate sense to Gerry, nor to Janet either. Mrs. Hospers came in to see what they were working on, and when Carl began to tell her what he had done, she stopped her ears.

"I don't want to hear it."

"Carl was helping the police, Mrs. Hospers. He had a right to be there. If he could see these files there, what's the big difference if he looks at them here?"

Mrs. Hospers looked at Gerry. "Try that one on Father Dowling."

After she had a little popcorn and stood watching Carl at his computer for a while, Mrs. Hospers decided that Mr. Walsh's records would be of work he'd done while he was still active. Since he was retired, it was like reading history.

"I think I could have lifted this off his computer sitting right here, Mom," Carl said, his nose inches from the screen.

"What do you mean?"

"His machine has a modem—it's always on; I call that number on my modem and I'm into his machine. There's probably a code needed to get at the files, but I think I could have figured it out."

"Carl!" Mrs. Hospers cried, looking at her son.

"I didn't say I'd do it, Mom. I don't have to. We've got the files. And like Gerry said, I'm helping the police."

Janet looked at Gerry and shrugged. It was something having a kid Carl's age know so much more about computers than they did. Gerry thought of the stories they'd heard, about hackers calling into the Pentagon computers, industrial theft, even bank robberies done by computer, the transfer of numbers from one account to another. Given the plight of her husband, Gerry didn't blame Mrs. Hospers for being alarmed by her son's electronic capacities. Still, the way she had raised her kids, he didn't think she had anything to worry about.

The control file that Carl had copied and now printed had a different name than the file that had been erased but the same extension, .CRO. The recovered file was called

D-MART.CRO. The control file was FLIGHT.CRO. They were both spreadsheets, and Gerry was struck by the similarity of the entries on the printout to those on the screen Carl was studying. Carl nodded when he mentioned this, and they began a methodical comparison.

"Maybe that's why he erased this file," Carl said. "It's just another version of that one."

"And slightly changed the name in the process?" Janet asked.

"Look, they're figures, right? Where are they added up?"

Carl hit a few keys, arriving at the bottom line. There was a noticeable difference between the amounts listed on the two files.

"Over a million-dollar difference," Janet breathed. "What does it mean?"

Carl didn't know. Gerry didn't know. But the thoughts he'd had about hackers earlier came back to him. Walsh was an accountant who had kept Crowe's books for him.

"Maybe he was stealing," Gerry said.

"D-MART.CRO has something the other doesn't," Carl said. "It looks like an account number."

He read it off, and Mrs. Hospers made Janet step back as she leaned over Carl's shoulder. "Read that out, Carl. I don't have my glasses."

Carl read it aloud as if it were a winning lottery number. Mrs. Hospers looked stunned. She stepped back from the computer.

"Mom, what's wrong?"

Mrs. Hospers was forming numbers with her lips. Then she let out a sigh. "That is almost identical with the account for the parish center. But not quite. What a relief."

Carl printed out the retrieved file too, despite his mother's urging him to go to bed. It was nearly eleven when

Gerry left, loaded down with the papers he was still holding when he stood in the doorway of the rectory study and let his uncle and Father Dowling know that he had found out something important.

"What's all that paper, lad?" Uncle Phil scowled at the printouts.

"Proof that Timothy Walsh was embezzling from Patrick Crowe."

If he had thrown a firecracker into the study the effect could not have been more dramatic. In moments they were in the dining room, with the papers spread out on the table. After a while there was the sound of Mrs. Murkin coming down the back stairway, and then she appeared at the kitchen door, clutching a floor-length robe about her, peering nearsightedly at the three of them.

"What are you doing in my dining room?"

The two men ignored her, so Gerry told her they were looking at printouts from Mr. Walsh's computer.

"Is there any news of that poor man?"

"No news, Marie," Father Dowling said. "Upstairs with you."

"Go get your beauty sleep," Captain Keegan said gruffly.

"It's obvious you've missed yours."

But the expected retort did not come. The printouts were too interesting. Marie shuffled off, climbing her stairway slowly, with audible complaints at the hardness of her lot.

The discrepancy between the bottom lines of the two files was the important thing. Just before that line was reached on D-MART.CRO a transfer had been made to the account number Mrs. Hospers had remarked was startlingly similar to the account of the parish center.

"Timothy Walsh volunteered to help Edna with her bookkeeping, Phil. She told him there wasn't much to it at all. After he looked at it, he agreed, and that was that."

"Look at the date of the transfer, Roger."

"That's just a week ago."

The two men were staring at one another when the phone rang. Marie got it before anyone downstairs could. Then she called, "Gerry. It's for you."

It was Carl. After the others had gone to bed, he had slipped back to his computer to see if he could tap into Walsh's.

"Somebody else was on, Gerry. Looking all over the place."

"At Mr. Walsh's?"

"Either that or phoning in the way I was."

"Thanks, Carl."

Gerry hung up, and when he repeated what Carl had told him, his uncle headed for the door. Father Dowling followed. What the heck. Gerry went along too. It was pretty clear that their destination was the apartment of Timothy Walsh.

22

Cy Horvath tried not to admit even to himself that he was putting in time over and above either regular or overtime, but he'd wanted to keep an eye on the Walsh apartment ever since he was there with Gerry. His wife expressed concern about the poor little man who had been kidnapped, no doubt treated a lot worse than the little old lady. Cy doubted that either Walsh or Agatha would like hearing the way Lydia described them. Edna Hospers and Marie Murkin worried about Walsh too, and if Phil Keegan didn't it was because he seemed sure the little accountant was doomed.

Cy found he wasn't that worried about Walsh. There was something about this that he couldn't put his finger on, but he was sure that if he could nothing would look the same. What was the motive for kidnapping Timothy Walsh? If Phil Keegan had taught him anything as a cop, it was that people do things for reasons, more often than not stupid reasons, but whatever they are, they are the explanations of what they do. So what reason did anyone have to snatch Walsh?

Sitting in his car on the quiet street, the seat pushed back as far as it could go so his legs didn't cramp up in the night air, he had all the time in the world to think it over. It turned out that Walsh had done accounting for D-Mart, which had been one of the outlets—innocent, of course—for the computers assembled from the parts stolen by Patrick Crowe. Walsh could have been in a spot to detect something funny in the origin of some of the store's merchandise. He seemed to have the kind of mind that would pursue a thought once he'd had it. So maybe he had discovered what Crowe was doing and then, like a good citizen, blew the whistle on the crook. Of course, one of his concerns would have been to protect a client, D-Mart. If Walsh had found out about Crowe, he could have found out about Fisk. So he made another phone call, and two bad characters were off the streets. Now, years later, Fisk shows up at the St. Hilary's parish center, to which Timothy Walsh almost daily comes to enjoy his retirement years and to flirt with ladies like Agatha. And then his computer is stolen, discovered by Fisk, returned, and everyone is happy.

Cy was certain that the missing computer was an important link. It was about the only event that tied Walsh and Willy Fisk together. What occurred to Cy Horvath was this: If Fisk suspected or had been told that Walsh's computer contained the explanation of his past troubles, he would have grabbed it to take a look.

There were several problems with that, however. First, Cy doubted that Fisk knew one thing about computers. Second, the machine hadn't been missing long enough for anyone who did understand computers to take a look at it.

So maybe it had been a failed attempt. Maybe when Walsh started yipping, Fisk got nervous and claimed to have found the thing. Someone just happened to stash it in the closet of the room where he was sleeping lest Patrick Crowe come scare him in the night. Sure. Not that Fisk or Crowe had to do the job themselves if they wanted to punish Walsh. But which one would do it? Either the two men were far better actors than Cy believed possible, or they were more like enemies than friends. If they didn't work together, they had to work separately. And nothing either of them had been up to suggested that a contact had been made with anyone else who might have put the snatch on Timothy Walsh.

A car turned into the street at the far corner and Cy prepared to slip out of sight, but the car was slowing down and then made a turn into the driveway of Walsh's apartment building. Cy had caught a glimpse of a small blue-and-gold sticker on the back bumper. Adobe: It was a rental car from the company Crowe worked for. Cy sat up and eased open his door.

Sounds in the night air carried and seemed closer than they were. He heard the door of the rental car open and shut. Footsteps and, after a moment, silence. Whoever it was had entered the building. Cy waited. From where he was he had a good view of the windows of Walsh's apartment. Two minutes went by, and his hopes that he had not waited in vain began to diminish. He settled back and was about to pull his door shut when the lights in Walsh's apartment went on. Cy was out of the car and across the street and inside the building in seconds. He tapped on the super's door, just keeping up a steady tattoo, until the door was opened. He had talked with Hazo earlier, but now the man's hair was wild on his head, he smelled of beer, and he looked as if he had fallen asleep watching television.

"I'm going upstairs to Walsh's apartment," Cy said, showing his ID. "Let me have a key."

Hazo turned and shuffled wordlessly across his room to a corkboard. He yawned as he stood in front of it, then took a key from its hook and shuffled back to Cy.

"You work nights too?"

"We never sleep."

"Neither do I."

Insomniacs, real or alleged, are worse than reformed drinkers for wanting to tell you the story of their lives. Cy nodded and headed for the stairs. Coming out of the stairwell would give him a greater chance of being unseen if someone were in the hallway. When an elevator door opened, there you were and there was nothing you could do about it. He had begun to feel tired sitting in the car but he felt great now, as if it were the beginning of the day, rather than the tail end. He would have no hesitation in letting himself into Walsh's apartment. Its occupant was a kidnap victim, and whoever was in there now would have a lot to explain.

On the third floor, he slowly opened the staircase door. The corridor was empty. He passed the entrance to Walsh's apartment and continued down the hall to another door. This would let him into the kitchen. The trouble with the back door was that it was seldom used, and no matter how gently Cy opened it, it let out an unoiled complaint. After what seemed minutes, he was inside, easing the door shut, having the same trouble doing it without making noise. Then he stood and listened. He heard what sounded like the tapping of computer keys. A rapid clicking, then a pause, then more clicking. It sounded like someone looking for something and not finding it.

Cy got out of his shoes and went carefully down the hallway. He could see the lights on in the front room; those were the lights he had seen from the street. Someone was in Walsh's study. The sound of the computer keys began again, and an expression of impatience. Cy had his gun out when he stepped into the doorway of the study. Patrick Crowe turned to look at him.

"Hi, Horvath. What took you so long? I noticed your car out front."

23

When Father Dowling arrived at Walsh's apartment with Gerry and Phil Keegan, it was to find Cy Horvath chatting with Patrick Crowe in the living room. Crowe seemed singularly unperturbed to have attracted such a crowd.

"The guy at my house call and tell you I was coming, Horvath?"

But nobody was going to give Crowe the satisfaction of knowing whether his guesses were accurate. Particularly since the stakeout at the halfway house had missed Crowe's departure.

"I'll ask the questions, Crowe. Where have you got Walsh?"

"Where? I wish I had that fink."

"Come on, you know what happened this morning. Who'd you have do it for you?"

Crowe laughed. "Shouldn't I have a lawyer?"

"You want to be arrested?"

"What else is going on here? I drop by to use a friend's computer and half the police department of Fox River drops by. Along with a chaplain. What's your role, kid?"

Gerry knew enough not to answer. Within ten minutes it was clear how the exchange would go. Cy and Keegan would try to get Crowe to answer questions about the missing

Walsh, while Crowe would insist that his visit was perfectly innocent. He had the owner's permission, he said.

"Look: I have a key."

"Where did you get that?" Cy asked, reaching for it. But Crowe's fingers closed around it and he withdrew his hand.

"I'd better get you home, Gerry," Father Dowling said, but he was at least as interested in getting himself back to the rectory. It had been silly to dash out with Phil Keegan as they had. If there was any constant theme of Phil Keegan's description of police work, it was that it was routine and thus dull. Father Dowling did not envy those who would have to spend hours fencing verbally with Patrick Crowe.

"Can't they make him tell them where Timothy Walsh is?"

The priest looked at Gerry. "Make him? No, of course not, if you mean use force. I wonder if Patrick Crowe even knows where Walsh is."

Gerry thought about that, but suddenly he yawned.

"I'm getting you home just in time."

Gerry went off to his room and Father Dowling, as was his habit, made a circuit of the first floor of the rectory in preparation for going upstairs himself. But he ended up in his study, filling his pipe with tobacco. If Gerry was right and Timothy Walsh had embezzled money from Patrick Crowe, that certainly seemed to put the little accountant in danger and provide a motive for kidnapping him. But turn it around: A free Patrick Crowe represented a threat to Timothy Walsh. Was it possible that Crowe did not yet know that he had been cheated by his accountant?

Father Dowling went into the dining room for the papers Gerry had brought home from the Hosperses' earlier. He was reminded of Gerry's story of Edna's reaction when she saw the number of the account into which Walsh had transferred a million and a half dollars but a few days ago. The pastor took the parish bankbook from his desk drawer. The accounts were one digit off. His hand moved hesitantly toward the phone, but then he decided, picked it up, and dialed. After several minutes a sleepy voice answered.

"Charles?"

"Who's that?" The sleepy voice had become angry.

"I'm sorry to be calling you at this hour, Charles. But it is important."

"Who is this?"

"Roger Dowling. Charles, I don't suppose you'd just have this kind of information in your head, but I wonder if a new account wasn't opened in your bank last week, an account in the name of the parish."

There was a subdued chuckle on the line. "I told him he wouldn't be able to keep it a secret from you."

"Timothy Walsh?"

"Did he decide to tell you after all?"

"Charles, I don't want to keep you up now. Perhaps you could explain it all to me sometime tomorrow. In the meanwhile, I'd like to ask you to stop anyone from withdrawing money from that account." Father Dowling consulted the printout and read off the numbers there.

"Is something wrong?"

"Let's talk in the morning. I mean anyone, Charlie. And that includes Timothy Walsh. I imagine you can tell if any attempt was made to transfer funds electronically, by way of a computer."

Charles Berglund was thoroughly awake now and would have been more than happy to be given a full explanation of this phone call. Father Dowling assured his banker that he would make everything clear on the morrow.

He hung up with the sense that he had closed one door.

But against whom? Everything Gerry and Janet had turned up seemed to the priest to point in one surprising direction. He had a good idea now who had kidnapped Timothy Walsh. Once more he made a circuit of the first floor of the rectory in preparation for turning in. From the window of the front room he looked toward the school. Something had momentarily caught his attention. There it was again. An outside night-light shone on the near wall of the building, but twice he had seen a change in a basement window.

He let himself out by the kitchen door and walked slowly toward the school. He told himself that this walk was just an extension of his circuit of the first floor of the house, a last check before going to bed. Of course he never included the school in this final tour, but what he had seen, or thought he had seen, at that basement window had to be looked into. Chances were it was nothing at all, a trick of lighting, perhaps simply his tired eyes misleading him. He went around to the front of the school and let himself in by the street door. It settled tightly into its frame behind him when he was inside, and then the great empty silence of the building enveloped him. He reminded himself that Willy Fisk would be in his bed on the third floor—surely the police had released him. Patrick Crowe had been released, only to be caught in Timothy Walsh's apartment. It was very unlikely that Crowe would see the halfway house again.

His crepe-rubber souls were noisy on the hallway floor and Father Dowling stopped, leaned against the wall, and took off his shoes. Coming over to the school at this hour was already odd. Carrying his shoes could not make it much odder.

He went down the flight of stairs at the opposite end of the school from the auditorium and then moved along the center of the unlit hallway toward the basement apartment.

Lights reflected many times off wall, ceiling, and doorway, palely illuminating the hall. At the door of the basement apartment he stopped and put his ear up against the panel. His first thought was that he would look very foolish if someone could see him. But of course no one could. He realized that he was holding his breath. And then he heard the sound. Water running.

He put his hand on the knob and turned it slowly. It did not give under pressure. He closed his eyes and visualized the apartment. He could think of no way an occupant could leave the apartment except through this hall door. He wondered if the fire inspector and insurance company had realized that. But they would not know that anyone was living here. He knocked sharply on the door.

"Timothy? It's Father Dowling. Open this door."

Perhaps this was the feeling people had when they bought a lottery ticket, or when they listened to the results on television. The risk had been taken, now would come the result. Millions of people every day lost at the lottery. He rapped again.

"Timothy," he said more loudly. "Open up."

And then he heard footsteps coming toward him. The bolt was moved and the door opened inwardly. At the same time the light in the apartment was turned on.

"Good evening, Father. Please come in."

Timothy Walsh stood there, a grim expression on his face. The gun in his hand was aimed at Father Dowling's chest.

24

"Where's Father Dowling?" Gerry asked.

It was the following morning, and he had just finished eating his breakfast in solitude, except for Mrs. Murkin popping in and out from her kitchen.

"Is he up?"

Gerry looked at her. "Oh, he's up and gone. His bed is made."

"Made!" Marie made an angry sound and bustled from the room, her voice trailing after her. "I told him I will make the beds, he doesn't know how to make beds, no man does. . . ."

Two minutes later, she was back. "That bed wasn't slept in. What time did you two get back?"

"I don't know. Late. I went right to bed."

"Father did come back with you, didn't he?"

"Sure. He seemed anxious to leave. We found Patrick Crowe prowling around in Timothy Walsh's apartment."

"You did!" Marie Murkin pulled out a chair and sat down, anxious to hear all about it. Gerry decided to tell the housekeeper about everything that had happened yesterday. He gave Carl Hospers most of the credit, but he wanted Marie Murkin to know that he and Janet and Carl had found out something that the police did not know. But Mrs. Murkin found it difficult to concentrate.

"I wonder if I should call your uncle."

"Why?"

"Gerry, the pastor isn't here. He did not sleep in his bed last night. I have no idea where he is. This has never happened before. I'm worried."

But Gerry thought of Father Dowling as he had last seen him and found it impossible to worry about him.

"He just got going early, Marie."

"I swear that the bed has not been slept in."

"Swear?"

He was kidding, but she seemed to wonder if she could be as sure as she pretended.

"Well, I've got to get to work. Especially if Father is already at it. Maybe there was a sick call and he had to go to the hospital."

Marie gave him a look. "I would have heard the phone."

"I didn't."

She was still thinking about that when he left. Going toward the school, aware of what a great summer morning it was, he told himself that it was good to be going to work. But he wouldn't mind running into Janet.

In the maintenance shed, through the opened doors, he saw the old people arriving for the daily programs. Mrs. Hospers's car was already parked in its usual place, and the van too was visible. Having gassed up the mower and checked the oil, Gerry was about to push it from the shed and get started when he thought, what the heck, it could be an hour before he even had a chance to see Janet. He stepped out of the shed and looked to see if Janet was visible among the groups forming for shuffleboard. He saw no sign of her, so he started across the playground to the gymnasium door.

Not finding her there, he thought she might be with her mother, so he went up the stairs two at a time. He nearly collided with Mrs. Hospers.

"Gerry, I'm trying to reach Father Dowling, and Marie tells me he's not at the house."

"He isn't."

Mrs. Hospers tucked in her chin. "Where is he?"

"I don't know. Marie thinks he didn't sleep in his bed last night. Of course, he might have fallen asleep reading in his study. I know he's done that before. I wonder if Marie looked there."

"Gerry, she was emphatic. She doesn't know where he is. The bank is calling, and Mr. Berglund wants to talk with Father."

"Where's Willy?"

"I'll call his apartment."

Mrs. Hospers hurried into her office and picked up the phone. Gerry headed for the stairs and bounded up to the third floor to the old nurse's office. He tapped on the door, then opened it and looked in. Fisk was in bed, sprawled on his back, his mouth open, snoring with abandon. Gerry shook his head and pulled the door closed.

Downstairs, Mrs. Hospers came out of her office. "Willy says he hasn't seen Father."

Gerry just looked at her. "You talked to him?"

She nodded, then rolled her eyes. "He must have had quite a night. He could hardly talk."

Gerry went back to the stairs, but this time went down—down to the basement and to the apartment. Whoever had answered Fisk's phone, it wasn't Fisk.

25

"It's no wonder Willy felt at home here, Father," Timothy Walsh said, looking around the basement apartment. "This must be very much like being in jail."

"Did Willy know the role you had played in sending him there?"

"He was guilty, Father. They caught him red-handed."

"Thanks to an anonymous tip."

"A citizen has his duties."

"You made it easy for the police to arrest Patrick Crowe too, didn't you? You made an awful lot of telephone calls, Timothy."

The dapper little man shifted the gun from one hand to the other. His mustache quivered as he adjusted his smile. "And you have made an awful lot of guesses."

"More recently you used the telephone to turn Patrick and Willy against each other. You have been a Judas, Timothy."

"Judas betrayed an innocent man."

"You stole from the thieves, didn't you? Manipulating the books, transferring funds?"

"Can stolen money be stolen, Father?"

"Oh yes. At least the attempt can be made. Fortunately, your attempt was foiled."

Timothy Walsh laughed. "Never con a con man, Father."

"It was not very imaginative of you to attempt to disguise your money in a St. Hilary's parish account. You will be unable to draw out any money, Timothy. Perhaps if you're lucky, they will put you in a cell as pleasant as this apartment."

What Walsh would have done if the phone had not rung then, Father Dowling could not have guessed. Walsh jumped at the sound, glaring at the phone and then at Father Dowling, as if the priest had made the phone ring. He edged toward it warily, lifted it, and brought it to his ear. Father Dowling could hear Edna's voice come over the wire.

"No, I haven't. No. Sorry." Walsh altered his voice as he spoke, then put down the phone.

"They're looking for you, Father."

"And also for you, Timothy. Why don't you put down that gun and accept defeat."

"Defeat!" The little man's eyes glittered defiantly. He backed toward the door, then stopped. There was a regretful expression on his face as he raised his arm. Father Dowling was looking directly into the barrel of the gun.

He began to murmur a Hail Mary, but the next sound he heard was not an explosion. The door burst open, catching Walsh from behind and propelling him across the room. Gerry came through the doorway and got behind Walsh, giving him a great shove. The little man teetered and danced, unable to regain his balance, and fell with a crash on the bed. The sound of the gun hitting the floor was music to Father Dowling's ears. He went to it, picked it up, and slipped it into his pocket. Then he picked up the telephone and jiggled the receiver.

"Edna? Would you call the police? Gerry has someone for them."

26

During the following week, Gerry was interviewed twice by newspaper reporters and appeared on the local news several times, not to mention the attention paid to the capture of Timothy Walsh on the networks' Chicago outlets. It did no good to say he had really done nothing, that they should really talk to Carl Hospers.

"Most people don't understand computers," Janet said. "But you knocked him down and tied him up and turned him over to the police."

"Probably saving Father Dowling's life," Mrs. Hospers added.

"Where is Carl?"

Edna and Janet groaned. "In his room with his computer, what else?"

Father Dowling had told Gerry not to mention the gun Timothy Walsh had threatened him with.

"He's in enough trouble without that, Gerry."

"He might have shot you."

"I don't think so. If he had, he would have missed."

"How can you be sure?"

"Did you ever play shuffleboard with him?"

Fisk was less interested in Gerry's heroics than in the fact that Timothy Walsh had ratted on him years ago and had been trying to get him sent back to Joliet.

"Never trust a man with a mustache, Gerry," Fisk instructed him.

"I'll remember that."

"You going to mow today?"

"Unless you want to."

Fisk pretended to give it some thought. "Naw, you go ahead."

It was good to be riding the tractor mower over the parish lawns, enveloped in its roar, able to think of recent events. All in all, he was glad he had come to Fox River for the summer.

Janet came out of the school and stood in its shade. He didn't let on that he saw her at first, but when he did look over, she was waving something. A Coke.

Not a bad idea. He cut the motor, got off the tractor, and started across the lawn toward Janet.